Pine Lakes Academy
News

Michael Dave

PINE LAKES ACADEMY NEWS

A NOVEL

Copyright © 2021 Michael Dave

All rights reserved.

ISBN-13:9798519620833

For Taylor first,

But also for Cooke, Seely, and Baker who are my favorite teachers after Mom.

CH 01

When Isaac Budgies stares into the cold reflective black lens of the camera, he knows he's gazing into the eyes and hearts of every teacher, student, staff, and guest of Pine Lakes Academy, grades first through eighth. From his broadcasting desk he can't see his reflection off the glass eyepiece, but Isaac imagines he's looking in the mirror. He smiles. The eighth grader's curly, almost blonde hair, looks both combed and yet as if he'd rolled out of bed without a shower. His school uniform buttoned-down collared shirt shows just a few wrinkles from under his sport coat, and his tie knot is exactly the right size.

"Thank you, Alyssa," he grins.

What comes next is so routine, so mechanical that it's become a mere reflex for Isaac Budgies. He's the longest running morning news anchor in the history of

Pine Lakes Academy. Isaac's been in front of the camera since sixth grade. Most news anchors, like the seasoned Alyssa Sonoma, don't start until seventh. His head bob, the tilt of the chin synchronized with the eyebrow raise, and finally, and—most crucial of all—his precise timing of the single click of the stack of papers that he will pick up and press together with both hands to make sure it hits the desk exactly as he says *news*. The whole school loved it. In fact, they expected it from him each and every morning, even Fridays:

"That's the morning *news*. Tomorrow, we'll tell you what we learned today."

Perfect, he says to himself.

Behind the glass, in the control room, eighth grader Cameron Chen whispers into his headset. Pine Lakes Academy has a strict uniform code, but Cameron's the type to wear a jacket and tie to school anyways, or at least a sweater vest. His jacket is flung behind his chair that he never sits in, revealing that he's wearing a short sleeve button-down shirt. His tie is loose and disheveled. It's a good thing he wears glasses. If Cameron couldn't nervously adjust those things on his eyes, and lose them on top of his stress-pulled black hair all day, he'd go nuts. The sound and effects girl, Zoe Vernar, sits next to him, but Cameron Chen is never one to do anything halfway, so he whispers into the mic to her and everyone else, "Fade to black."

"And queue signature," Chen orders.

Zoe presses the button her hand was already hovering over, and the black screen displays a stamped colorful Pine Lakes Academy News logo that Zoe designed herself.

The logo read:

PINE LAKES
ACADEMY
🌎 NEWS 🌎
Today's date: Thursday, August 27th

"Kill the microphones," Cameron said. Then, mimicking a conductor, "Bring in music."

Zoe turns the knob to summon the background audio.

Cameron takes his headset off while proudly saying in his inside voice, "And we're out."

The "On Air" light from inside the studio shuts off. Isaac Budgies claps for the whole newsroom team, which includes: himself and Alyssa Sonoma as anchors, the three camera operators, a rookie seventh grade weather girl, and a producer sitting between cameras 1 and 2. Chen has to walk out of the control room, into the library, then through the studio door before he can chime in on the congratulations. It always bothered him that Isaac got to be the first to applaud the team. But Cameron often reminded himself that Isaac was really only praising Isaac; it was Cameron who spoke to the crew.

"Another great show everybody," Cameron says without closing the studio door behind him, "Brilliant."

"Chocolate chip cookies? How did I mess up saying chocolate chip cookies?" Jenny Towlel asked. She's the rookie, standing behind the green chroma key curtain. Earlier in the broadcast, she fumbled through the lunch menu and thought about nothing since.

"It was fine, Jen. It was great," Cameron calmed her. "You smiled and didn't put a spotlight on it. You handled it perfectly."

"Did I though?"

"I'm going to keep a recording of it and show it to all the recruits in a training video," Cameron speaks with his hands. "It was the flawless way to make a mistake."

"It helps if you aren't nervous," Alyssa Sonoma says with her hand out and admiring her red fingernails. She wouldn't dare admit this to anyone in the world, but she was already feeling slightly threatened by Jenny Towlel. The newsroom's a crowded cast, and there's only room for one pretty face. Alyssa decided she didn't like Jenny, and she decided she wasn't going to change her mind about it either. She wondered what Isaac thought about the weather girl. Of course, Isaac wouldn't be threatened by her, so Alyssa presumed Isaac hadn't thought about her at all.

Mr. Docker walks into the room clapping, "Well done everybody, well done."

Mr. Docker has long grey hair that he wears slicked back in a tangled mess. Mr. Docker is the teacher sponsor behind PLAN. He's tall and thin, and his wire-framed glasses sit low on his long nose. "Nice job everyone, nicely done. Jennifer, don't sweat the cookies thing."

"Oh great you noticed?" She pulls at her ponytail, "Was it that bad?"

"Enough with the cheese and crackers thing, can we talk about the election, please?" Isaac Budgies was all business and still seated at his anchor chair.

Alyssa had since gotten up, regretting it now that Chen was sitting next to Isaac; they had the floor.

They're in complete control of the room now, she thought. *Ugh, why did I get up from my seat?* Alyssa wondered if Isaac waited to make a good point until after she'd gotten up. *Probably.*

"Yes," Chen chimes in, "We need to talk about angles, sides, controversies. This is going to be one of the most heated elections in the history of the school."

"We don't have enough time right now. You all need to get to first period," Mr. Docker says looking at his rectangular watch. It doesn't have any numbers or symbols on its face, only a gold dot for the 12.

There's no way he can actually read that thing, Chen thinks.

"We'll discuss it in class," Docker says.

Budgies and Chen exchange looks. They both wanted to talk about the election now, with the core team only. The Advanced News class, taught by Mr. Docker, would have sixth and seventh graders in there too. Chen and Budgies both agreed election coverage was far too delicate a science to talk in front of the entire class. Their looks told each other they'd have their own meeting during second period algebra.

Urgh, Alyssa grunts to herself. She sees the look and knows what those two are thinking. She's not in algebra. *And so what if I'm in remedial math? It's not remedial; it's average.* She'll have to get filled in by Isaac during gym class. Which means she'd have to talk to Isaac in public. She hated doing that.

"We'll need to get a jump on the candidates," Alyssa said.

She was not about to let the first big story of her eighth grade year fall into the hands of Isaac Budgies. "Like, obviously it's going to be Glenda, Macie, and Jeff."

"Jeff Barringer isn't going to run," Isaac said as casual as possible putting on his backpack.

"Oh my gosh, what?" Jenny Towlel asked. "He's the most popular guy in eighth grade."

"Second most, maybe," Isaac said. The implication was for himself as first. He looked around the room for a laugh but didn't see any.

"How do you know he's not running?" Alyssa asked.

Did I hide the shock behind my voice? Alyssa was in Jeff's clique. Jeff Barringer wasn't even friends with Budgies. *Since when does Jeff talk to Isaac before me?*

"A little bird told me," Isaac Budgies said. "Says he's going to focus on his band. Maybe he realized getting involved with student governance isn't on-brand to the rock star reputation he's cultivating."

"Okay that's enough for now," Mr. Docker says holding the door open to imply the meeting is over and the school day has officially begun. "The election is going to be a big story for us. I can feel it. I will see you all at sixth period. Out."

The students shuffled out of the classroom. Isaac delayed. He's intentionally trying to be the last out the door. Cameron noticed, so he stayed in his seat.

"Jenny," Isaac said quietly tilting his head back signaling for the seventh grader to lag behind.

"Oh gosh, am I in trouble?"

Isaac faked a laugh. He shook his head. Mr. Docker sensed the learning moment approaching and left the room without comment. Isaac sat down back in his normal anchor spot to demonstrate something. Cameron remained silent next to him.

"The first few times I sat here, I was so nervous I sat on my hands the whole time like this, stiff as a robot."

"Really?" she asked.

"Don't I look ridiculous with my arms down at my sides?"

"Yeah," Jenny laughed. "You really did that?"

"Yes. Because everybody does something embarrassing on camera when they're new. But you'll get used to it."

"Thanks, Isaac," Jenny smiled and walked out the door.

Cameron waited for the door to shut all the way.

"You've never once sat on your hands for a broadcast," he said.

"Yeah, but she doesn't need to know that," Isaac shrugged.

CH 02

Isaac and Cameron walk down the hallway together towards their algebra class. Classes started several minutes ago. They're the only two in the hallway. One of the hall monitors stops them. Mr. Potam is a giant. He's about six and a half feet tall, as big as a rhinoceros compared to the students of Pine Lakes.

"Hey, where do you two think you're going?" Mr. Potam grunts.

"We have Algebra," Isaac grins.

"Great show today, guys," Mr. Potam says. He doesn't care at all that they're late. Most students would get in trouble for loitering in the hallways between periods. Isaac Budgies and Cameron Chen are in all advanced courses, and loved by the faculty and staff. This interaction proves once again that the rules don't seem to apply to the school's minor celebrities and shining stars.

"Oh by the way," he snorts after they start walking away. "Isaac, are you going to run for council president?"

Cameron instinctively lets out an irritated sigh, surprising himself that it came out. But, he knows exactly how Budgies is going to answer the question.

"Na," Isaac says, pretending to be humble, but the smirk on his face gives it away.

"Really?" He rocks back from the response. "But you'd win. There's no chance you wouldn't win."

Cameron can see Isaac's head getting bigger. *Here it comes*, Cameron thinks to himself, *his new favorite joke.*

"I can't give up the best seat in the house," he smiled.

"Oh that's right, rule 19.8.4. Well, we wouldn't want you to stop doing the news," Mr. Potam scratches his head with an elephant trunk of an arm.

There is a rule in the Pine Lakes Academy student constitution, famously Paragraph 19, section 8.4, often referred to as the Orwell law. It prohibits student council presidents from participating in the PLAN broadcast program. The theory behind the rule is the school media should not be directly involved with those who have the authority to create school policies.

Rule 19.8.4 protected students against a biased news source, and also served the practical purpose of preventing the adolescent minds of 12 and 13 year-olds from thinking they ruled the world. Isaac Budgies could have a sweeping victory from a unanimous sixth grade vote alone, but he took too much pride in the news to risk throwing it away for a presidency. Besides, he often wondered what exactly an eighth grade president even does or why it's important at all.

"I need to focus on my career," Isaac explained.

The hall monitor chuckled and let them pass without any further hindrance. He didn't even bother pointing out to them that they were taking the long way to get to Algebra.

"You didn't tell him the other two reasons," Cameron added.

"What do you mean?" Isaac tried to laugh off Chen's comment, but the sound that came out of his mouth most closely resembled a cough.

"Oh come on. I'm your best friend. I know the real reason why you're not running," Chen explained. "Sure, you'd probably get the celebrity votes from sixth and seventh grades and that's enough to win, but would you really want to be a president who can't win his own grade?"

"Kids our age are too worried about nonsense. I don't have time to make friends," Isaac explained, "And neither do you, pal," Budgies reminded Cameron.

"And what about Alyssa?" Chen probed. "You wouldn't risk your one and only chance at your dream girl—current dream girl—I should say. That's the main reason you're staying on PLAN."

"Hey, I love the news. You know that. I was on PLAN before Alyssa got there," Isaac started to get defensive. He looked around to ensure it's still only them in the hallway.

"Yea, but now she's there, and she's all you care about."

Isaac blushed.

"See?" Chen laughed, "You're obsessed, man. Just admit it."

"Well, so what? Who wouldn't be? She's popular, pretty, smart, and she's good at the news."

"She's not smart," Chen rebutted.

"Well, maybe not smart like Zoe. But she's sharp, maybe. I mean, so what she's not the best with word problems, or computers, but she's got wit. She's funny on-air."

"I write her jokes," Cameron said. "She reads those from the teleprompter."

"Well, she's got great delivery, okay?"

"Good luck," Chen shrugged. "Zoe has friends who like you."

"We can't all be dating Zoe, can we? And I don't want to go out with Zoe's friends. I want to go out with Alyssa Sonoma, and I will."

"We've spent all this time talking about Alyssa, we didn't say anything about the election," Chen swiped his hand through is black hair in frustration and it stood straight up afterwards. "Get focused on our priority."

"I am. I am." Isaac promised.

"You better be," Chen pointed his index finger at his best and probably only real friend. "This election is going to be one of the most controversial of all time, and we need to cover it. We'll go down as the best news duo in school history. This kind of stuff goes on a college admission essay. So focus."

"You're right, you're right. Sorry. I'm focused. I'll be a professional. No girl, not even Alyssa Sonoma, is going to jeopardize my unprecedented third year as Pine Lakes Academy News's best anchor. You can count on that."

"Speaking of counting," Chen looks at his watch; it's digital. "We're thirteen minutes late."

CH 03

Mr. Docker's been teaching PLAN for years, recruiting kids who show interest as early as fifth grade. He even has "PLAN Broadcast Training" set up as part of the advanced placement program for sixth grade and up.

Unlike most classrooms with a chalkboard, PLAN Broadcasting uses a corkboard. Mr. Docker stands in front of the giant corkboard and pins up a notecard that read:

Student Council President Election

"Well?" Mr. Docker asks the class, "Where is our story? What is our angle? The nominees go live on Monday; where are we?"

Mr. Docker looked passed Chen and Budgies for answers to the rest of the class. PLAN was the only class where Isaac didn't sit in a middle side seat. Whenever given the choice, Isaac felt the middle and side was actually the best place to sit. People trying too hard to be cool sat in the back, and nerds sat in the front. Sitting in the middle allowed him to be on the fringe of both groups: Teachers thought he was smart and students think he's cool. In every class except PLAN, Cameron sits behind Isaac, so Isaac can't copy off him.

But in PLAN class, Isaac sits front and center with Cameron and Alyssa on either side of him. In PLAN, there was often a lot of debate, and Cameron and Isaac found by sitting in the front and talking quietly they could easily exclude the younger class members who sat behind them. Isaac glanced to Alyssa. Alyssa hated sitting up front, and even more so, being seen sitting next to Isaac. Everyone in school always assumed they were dating. She worried Isaac was beginning to think they were too. But she had to sit up front, because those two talk so quietly, it's the only way she can get in on the conversation.

Oh gosh, she thought to herself. *Is this a "he likes me" look or is this a "do I know the answer to the question" look? I wish he didn't like me. Now Cameron's looking at me, I wish he didn't hate me. Fine.* Alyssa raised her hand.

"Yes, Alyssa?" Mr. Docker asked with his black sharpie ready to go on the next notecard to be pinned to the board.

"There's like two main candidates; that's obvious. Macie Neadle is like the classic popular vote—and also like one of my best friends, so let's watch what we say about her," Alyssa said this looking at both Cameron and Isaac. "And like her main competition is Glenda Howard. She's like the responsible nerdy vote. Like we should focus on these two as the main nominees."

Six, Cameron thought to himself. He held up as many fingers to Zoe. He liked counting Alyssa's "likes."

"Excellent," Mr. Docker tacked a notecard for each candidate on opposite sides of the board. After being the head of Pine Lakes Academy News for nearly two decades, Docker wasn't one easily surprised by stories. Docker had both Glenda Howard's and Macie Neadle's school photos from the year before. He pinned them up under their respective names. It was his nonchalant preparedness that impressed the students most. Obviously, Docker knew which names were going to be the main candidates; asking the class was more of a rhetorical question.

Glenda Howard: eighth grader, cross-country team, chess team, advanced algebra and science courses, and an amazing cello player. She wore both glasses and braces, and was an ethnic melting pot; she was virtually the perfect political candidate for class president. She wasn't popular, but well known throughout the school with a solid reputation. In ten months from now, everyone knows she'll be delivering the graduation speech as valedictorian.

Macie Neadle: also an eighth grader, represents the classic snotty popular girl trying to prove she was more popular than snotty. She has thick sandy brown hair, bright blue eyes, and is anatomically advanced for her age. Cameron once joked to Isaac that if Macie Neadle kept her brains in her bra strap she'd be a double genius. Macie is on the dance team. She took average classes and got average grades, participated in no other extracurricular activities, but she was the most famous girl in school. She was even more popular than Alyssa, which Alyssa was secretly jealous about. Actually, Alyssa's the only person who thinks her secret jealousy is a secret.

Docker pinned up both the pictures, and then took a step back to think with his hand on his chin, "And what is our main angle for covering each candidate? Do we know where they stand on the issues? Ah, which brings me to the issues."

Isaac Budgies raised his hand, but he started talking before he was called on, "We're leaving out a third contender."

Mr. Docker turned a little red in the face, and scratched the back of his ear.

"What do you mean a third contender, Isaac?" Mr. Docker asked. "I agree with Alyssa, the race will come down to these two. We need to start preparing for it now."

"Moose Patrowski is running," Isaac responded.

The class gasped and whispered.

"We didn't know about this. Are you sure?" Mr. Docker asked, this time sounding like he was actually asking a question and didn't already know the answer.

"A little bird told me," Isaac shrugged.

Where does Isaac Budgies get these little birds? Alyssa wondered to herself.

The class was in a frenzy over the news. Whispers and gasps about the late candidate hummed the classroom. Students had up until the end of the day to throw their names in the hat, and Moose was a fairly popular student, an eighth grade jock.

"He didn't tell me that," Jenny Towlel, the seventh grader chimed in over the buzz. What a golden opportunity she missed by not being the one to divulge this story. Jenny was in a very tight circle with Moose. They were cousins; it was a family circle. She wondered why he hadn't told her himself. She just saw him over the weekend too. He said nothing.

"This will be our first announcement tomorrow," Chen spoke over the buzz. "Moose will pull votes from both Glenda and Macie. There's no way to predict who could win this race now."

"Do you actually think Moose has a chance?" Alyssa worried for her frenemy. But if she was being perfectly honest with herself, perhaps she hoped a little that Macie would indeed lose the race. *It would devastate Macie. Am I smiling?*

Mr. Docker didn't have Moose's picture to stick up onto the board. He had to write his name on a card in the middle. He didn't like being out-informed by one of his students.

Moose was a bit of a class clown, but a budding talent at Pine Lakes. Famous for wearing a fake mustache, and starring in the school plays, he was also the starting center on the eighth grade basketball team since sixth grade. Moose was already over six feet tall, had auburn hair, and brown eyes. He was simply addicted to the spotlight. If he had the grade requirements, Moose Patrowski would probably be siting in Alyssa's spot in the morning broadcast. He would surely garner several votes.

"He probably won't win," Chen explained, speaking with the wisdom of an old man, despite this being only the third election he's covered.

"But," Zoe Vernar spoke for the first time; she sat on the other side of Cameron. The two took pride in their professionalism, probably only half the underclassmen had any idea they were dating. During school hours the couple was strictly business. People didn't know much about Zoe, generally. As a default, she was aloof to everyone. She had a single streak of pink down one side of her otherwise blonde hair, very much against school policy, but even teachers seemed too intimidated by her to bring this to anyone's attention. What if she didn't take it out?

"He is going to make it almost impossible to predict between Glenda and Macie. If he takes it seriously," Zoe said about Moose.

"I agree. This complicates things, Zoe." Docker snapped his fingers. "Budgies, you'll break the story tomorrow at the top of the hour. Then we'll do a teaser, shoot it over for lunch and weather, and get back into the election coverage with the issues. What are the issues?"

Jenny Towlel raised her hand, Docker pointed at her to answer. Isaac also raised his hand and once again, spoke without waiting to be called on. "School lunch program, field trip funding allocation, and uniforms."

The room murmured amongst itself again at the word *uniforms*. Jenny only sunk in her chair, counting another lost speaking opportunity to the great and powerful Isaac Budgies.

"Uniforms?" Someone from the back echoed. "Don't we have to wear uniforms?"

"Moose's main platform is going to be rolling back the school's uniform policy," Isaac grinned. "Did you know that?" He asked half turning towards Jenny.

How could she have known? Jenny didn't have access to Isaac's secret spreading little birds. *But at least he's talking to me!* Jenny thought.

Alyssa wondered why he didn't aim the insult at her instead. She would have rather been insulted than ignored.

"Can he do that?"

"Is that allowed?"

"I hate uniforms!"

And so on and so forth.

"That could get interesting," Alyssa admitted.

"How long does the campaigning last?" Jenny Towlel asked.

"Two weeks," Chen, Vernar, Sonoma and Budgies all answered in unison.

"Let's focus now, everyone," Mr. Docker snapped his fingers three times. "We have a lot to cover. This election will certainly be one of the most exciting this school has seen in years. We need to make sure we are hitting it from every possible angle."

Mr. Docker always did that: exaggerated. Everything was always "the most exciting ever," or "most anticipated of all time." He overstates as a way to teach his students to always build the hype. He has a whole lesson plan on it they will cover later in the year. "The news, first and foremost," he often says, "is entertainment."

CH 04

"As we're now a few days into this election, Isaac, it sure seems like things are heating up. Have you decided who you'll vote for?" Alyssa looked at him and gave him her on-screen smile, teeing him for their next segue. On the air, they had great chemistry.

"That's right, Alyssa. It sure is a tight race right now. I'm still undecided. Hopefully, after this afternoon's long awaited debate, I'll be a little more clear." Then he turned from her to camera-one, "But I understand you were able to catch-up with some of the students around the building to see who they're supporting?

For whom, Cameron corrected Isaac mentally from inside the booth.

"Load video feed one; prepare for jump cut," he instructed Zoe.

"That's right Isaac, and here's what the rest of Pine Lakes Academy had to say about their picks for student council president."

"Jump cut to video feed," Cameron said inside the booth.

Zoe pressed the buttons to switch the monitors from Alyssa's smile to a breakaway clip. She knows what to do; Cameron's instructions are just background noise to her.

"Play video."

The on-location footage opened with shots of Moose Patrowski walking around the school in a fake mustache, knocking on first and second grade classrooms passing out little badges to wear that said, "Can't lose with Moose." They had a picture of Moose Patrowski's face with moose antlers on his head. Then the video cut to some sixth graders standing outside by their lockers.

"I mean, like, *lose* and *Moose* don't even rhyme," a girl in pig tails said. "And you can't even vote until sixth grade."

"I think he's funny," another girl in the group with messy hair said. "I'm voting for Moose."

Then another cut to some older eighth graders: two boys and girl, all with their uniforms freshly pressed and books in hand walking out of a classroom.

"This isn't a popularity contest," the girl with glasses said, clenching her books to her chest. "Glenda Howard is going to make sure that all grades get the most funding for field trips, and I really like her plan for budgeting for new computers in the library."

"Most definitely, Glenda Howard," a skinny boy with long hair said. "I mean look at this girl. She is a true class act."

The camera panned over to see Glenda Howard down the hall sharing a genuine laugh with the big hall monitor, Mr. Potam.

"Nobody cares more about this school than Glenda. Glenda's the way," the student said on camera.

Next, the footage cut to eighth grade basketball phenom, Lance Wallace. He was in the gym, with his gym uniform sleeves cut short to reveal his muscles. He drained a three-pointer.

"Hey, Moose is my teammate, but let's make it interesting. If I make it, I'll vote for Macie, a miss and I'll vote for Moose."

Lance swished another three-pointer, "Sticking with Macie I guess," he said raising his palms and shrugging.

Finally, a group of seventh grade boys sat around their lunch table and they all climbed over each other to get face time on the camera. They pointed and pulled at their shirts to reveal all of them were wearing jaguar printed "Macie fur Prez" pins.

Thanks to Zoe's perfect execution in the control room, the feed cut back seamlessly to Alyssa, who waited with a smile, frozen in place like a professional robot.

"Well, Isaac I don't know about you, but I think it still seems too close to call. You're not the only one undecided. After the debate this afternoon, we'll have a better idea of where the students are leaning." She said through her burning cheeks.

"I hope so Alyssa, but we've still got one more week to go."

"Don't forget, students," Alyssa chimes back in, and the screen zooms in on just her now. "Today's debate is at 1:45 pm. All students, grades sixth through eighth, are to report to the auditorium at 1:40 pm. Back to you, Isaac."

The broadcast jump cuts to Isaac, he pauses.

"Thanks Alyssa. That's the morning news. Tomorrow, we'll tell you what we learned today."

At 12:02 PM, the fire alarm went off. As usual, most of the kids in the building took the sound of the alarm for permission to pull out their phones and resume conversations with friends, even the friends in the same classroom as them. Teachers stood up to keep everyone calm; nobody cared. This was probably a drill.

Standard operating procedure for a fire drill was to exit and head to the back of the school, near the bus turnaround. This is also where the second graders conducted recess. Once the mass of students started to make their way outside, the laughter and awes shot back to those still trickling through the hallway. Isaac, Cameron, and Zoe rushed to get outside to pull out their phones and take pictures.

"Zoe, are you getting this?" Cameron asked.

"Unbelievable," she said panning across with her phone camera.

Moose Patrowski arranged all the second graders to stand outside with homemade banners and posters. The youngsters in their sweater vests held out "Can't Lose with Moose" posters along with several other creative jabs at his opponents.

"The Monster under my bed dresses as Macie Neadle for Halloween"

"Glenda Howard's favorite food is π"

"Macie Neadle thinks times tables are furniture"

And others that were similar, but not as funny.

The entire Pine Lakes Academy student body now thought that the fire drill was a set-up.

"Was this planned? This is classic," Budgies said.

"We'll need to start finding out who pulled the alarm," Chen's mathematical mind fired out. "The teachers will be looking to get to the bottom of this."

"I'm getting verified reports that Moose Patrowski was already outside for lunch when the alarm went off. He must have had someone to help." Zoe said capturing the cute little kids holding up their signs and reading texts.

"Well, don't jump to conclusions," Isaac smirked. "Anyone paying attention long enough would know there's always a fire drill within the first couple weeks of school."

Cameron read Budgies' face like a children's book. Isaac practically confessed to being involved with this fiasco.

But why? And more importantly, why didn't my best friend tell me about this?

Probably because Cameron would try talking him out of it; or because this was just too good of news for Cameron not to come prepared with a camera, which would tip off their involvement in the whole thing. Cameron agreed with his own reasoning.

Am I that untrustworthy? I wish he'd tell me this kind of crap, Cameron asked himself, adjusting his glasses.

"Haha, look at this one," Zoe's laugh snapped Cameron out of his inner dialog. She pointed to a little girl holding up a sign that said: "Macie Neadle Can't Right in Cursive."

Cameron laughed too, but not at the joke. He knew it was Isaac's joke. He laughed at the fact Isaac put so much effort into trying to sway the election. The real news story would be exposing Isaac. But friends don't do that sort of thing. *Guys don't, anyway*, he reckoned. Zoe would be very mad at him if she heard him think that.

"Funny a dumb kid like Moose would make a joke about not using the right *write*," Cameron raised an eyebrow to let Isaac know he was upset. "Almost makes you think he must have had a friend who *told him*! about that."

"That's the beauty of it. He doesn't care," Budgies laughed. "Oh my gosh look, take a pic."

Macie Neadle was not pleased about being outdone. She walked outside with her hands on her hips and lips pressed together. Alyssa, and the rest of Macie's loyal and less attractive associates, stood in a circle refusing to look at the clever banners. Isaac got in closer to take a picture. He also made sure to take a picture of Glenda Howard.

Like a veteran politician, Glenda found the cleverest poster held up by the cutest little boy and posed for Isaac to take a picture. Glenda, with her dark curly hair tied back, scrunched down next to the little second grader and his sign that said: "Glenda Howard does homework during recess." She gave two-thumbs up.

CH 05

Cameron reached his boiling point. As the fire department directed the students inside, he grabbed Isaac and used his electronic student ID fob on the rear auditorium entrance. Most students' identification cards wouldn't work on this door because it goes directly backstage of the theatre. In fact, no students' identification cards are supposed to work on this door.

"Hey, what's going on, man?" Isaac asked while Cameron took his arm.

"Don't talk to me until we get in the room."

Last year, as advanced members of the seventh grade broadcast team, Isaac and Cameron often needed access to the color printer in Mr. Docker's office in the library. They asked Docker to use the printer so many times that he finally put in a request to the Tech Department to upgrade Isaac and Cameron's ID fobs to grant them access to the office so they could print themselves. What nobody in the Tech Department, or Mr. Docker, realized was that the change inadvertently upgraded Isaac and Cameron's ID cards to "faculty" status on all electronic locks in the building.

Cameron and Isaac swore to never reveal the error to anyone else. Cameron told Zoe the next day, but Isaac assumed he would. When it came to Cameron and Isaac's many secrets, "not telling anyone else" implied to both of them, "except Zoe."

The two used their security perk mostly to get into the faculty men's bathroom in the music department. Pine Lakes only had female music teachers, so Isaac and Cameron used it as their private meeting room on occasions such as this. The fastest way to get into the bathroom was through the auditorium, which was also cut-off from student entry, but they used their key cards to get in there too.

"What the heck is going on with you?" Isaac blurted as soon as they shut the door in the private bathroom.

Despite their anger, they both ducked down out of habit to make sure the stalls were in fact unoccupied.

"I could ask you the same question," Cameron said.

"What, the fire alarm? You think I had anything to do with that?" Isaac blushed, and walked to the furthest urinal away from Cameron.

"Are we best friends or not?"

The question caught Isaac off-guard.

"Yeah man, what's going on with you?"

"I want to know why you are deliberately keeping me out of your plan to rig this election," Cameron said.

"Rigging the election? What are you tal—"

"—Cut the crap, Budgies. I'm smarter than you. Are you going to tell me your plan or not?"

Isaac took a deep breath. The harder he fought not to smile, the bigger his grin grew. He was a professional exaggerator, but not very good at lying. "Okay."

"Ugh, I knew it!" Cameron said. "Why wouldn't you tell me about this? How long have you been planning it?"

"Slow down Cam, you're going to have a heart attack. I didn't think you'd want to be involved."

"You are so transparent," Cameron smirked. "This, this whole thing is so, so ... obvious to me." Cameron washed his hands. "You're like a delusional cartoon character."

"Oh you're a physiatrist now?" Isaac scoffed.

"I just think it's pretty pathetic for a guy whose head is already the size of Mount Rushmore to try and deliberately prevent his crush's best friend from winning a junior high election. This whole thing is Zoe's fault, isn't it?"

Budgies didn't answer.

Cameron had a memory flashback: Just a week or two before the school year started, the three of them were talking about eighth grade, and what they expected would be the big stories of the year. Naturally, they discussed the election and how Macie would win. It was then, that Isaac mentioned he hoped he would be able to date Alyssa before the end of the year. Zoe just had to open up her mouth and explain how that was going to be impossible if Macie won student council president.

According to Zoe, in the popularity contest between Alyssa and Macie, winning class president would be very hard for Alyssa to top. Zoe predicted if Macie won a presidential title, Alyssa would probably try to date someone in high school, or do something equally drastic to keep their popularity struggle even. She certainly wouldn't date someone like Isaac, who although was well known, was not actually popular in the traditional sense.

This was all perfectly believable to Cameron. He chalked it up as an immature and irrational thought process. However, what surprised him was that apparently Isaac believed the utter nonsense. And even more shocking, Isaac must have stewed on that conversation ever since. Over the last few weeks, Isaac evidently concocted his absurd ploy to prevent Macie from winning.

"So what did you think?" Cameron continued.

"Macie will lose and so then all the sudden Alyssa will want to date you because it will make you two an on-screen power couple or something?"

"Okay, that's enough," Isaac spoke to Cameron's reflection through the mirror. "See? This is why I didn't want to get you involved."

"Hey, whatever psycho twisted plan you have to make Alyssa Sonoma—who is a total birdbrain by the way—*finally* fall in love with you, be my guest." Cameron lowered his voice and said, "I just wish you'd tell your best friend, and more importantly, your Producer-Director about rigging an election."

"I'm not rigging the election," Isaac rolled his eyes. "I'm just making it interesting. Let's face it: it's no good for our story if all we have is the cliché popular girl winning out against the smart nerdy girl."

Before Cameron could respond, Isaac continued, "Plus, it's kind of my way of getting back at the school for their stupid rule. I should be the one winning this election."

"There it is!" Cameron clapped. "The truth comes out. You want to be the school president? After all your BS-ing about how you don't care about the rule; how you've got 'the best seat in the house?' I knew you wanted to be in the election."

"Of course I did. Okay? So what?"

"Now answer me this: Do you actually want to be

the school president? Or do you just want to win the election?"

Isaac laughed, "Well what do you think, doctor?"

"I will give you credit at least for convincing Jeff Barringer to drop out of the race."

"Thank you. I casually let him overhear one comment. Let it marinate for a couple days. Then randomly asked him if he was officially *becoming a suit* and he dropped the idea on the spot. Easy."

"Yeah, that's pretty easy. He wouldn't have won, but definitely would have robbed votes from Glenda."

"Exactly."

"But," Cameron went on, "What I don't understand is why you'd choose Moose Patrowski as the Manchurian Candidate?"

"You said it yourself, man," Isaac Budgies shrugged. "Ego."

Cameron rolled his eyes.

"Well from this moment on, can we do it together?" Isaac asked.

Cameron paused for a second. He pulled at his hair, and did some calculating.

He adjusted his glasses. "Do I think you have a chance with Alyssa Sonoma? No."

"Noted."

"But, ultimately, what do I actually care about who wins? An eighth grade president doesn't do anything. It does make the election a much more interesting race." Cameron shrugged. "Tomorrows need headlines too."

Isaac reached out his hand for a shake.

"Wash it first," Cameron smiled.

CH 06

No one but Mr. Docker would be more suitable to play moderator for the election debate. The auditorium set up three podiums on one side, with Docker sitting behind a desk on the other. He and the candidates faced forward to the crowd.

Rightfully so, Cameron thought, *these 'candidates' look more like game show contestants. This whole election is just one big game now. A game that Isaac and I plan on winning. But what's the prize?* Cameron wondered. *Robbing Glenda Howard of a rightfully owned presidency? No, that's not it; unfortunately, she can't win. It will be protecting the school from someone like Neadle. Girls like Glenda never win these elections when they're up against ruthless girls like Macie. And look at Isaac over here.*

Isaac sat next to Cameron, on the opposite side of Zoe, looking around the auditorium.

Did he find her yet? Cameron wondered, knowing that Isaac's eyes scanned the room for Alyssa.

I'm kind of happy she doesn't like him. Is that wrong? Gosh, I wish Zoe never put this whole thing in his head. Wait till I tell Zoe about this one!

Cameron ultimately agreed to help Isaac with helping an imbecile like Moose Patrowski win the election because Cameron agreed it might prevent Macie from winning. A potential class president like Moose was harmless, whereas someone like Macie didn't deserve to win. She was mean, selfish, and seemed to enjoy making other people feel bad about themselves. So for those reasons, he'd help Isaac, but certainly not for Isaac's ridiculous pursuit of Alyssa. That whole thing still made zero sense to Cameron, but he always deferred to Zoe when it came to the minds of teenage girls.

I just don't get what he sees in her, Cameron said again as he and Isaac spotted Alyssa entering the theater. *She is not interesting. Other than being really good at smiling and reading aloud, she has no skillset.*

Cameron's memory flashed him back to third grade:

Mrs. McDarnad's third grade classroom had linoleum-tiled floors. The desks could never quite stay where they were supposed to be. The chrome legs with those ball and socket jointed desk stoppers on the bottom slid around on the white and speckled tiles. Cameron sat next to Alyssa in third grade. Even then, at eight years old, Alyssa knew she'd grow up to be a beautiful girl. Cameron laughed thinking that the last thing some girls ever care to learn is that they're pretty. At least, he thought so, anyway.

Do I sound bitter? He wondered as he continued with his flashback.

On the day Cameron decided he'd never like Alyssa Sonoma, Mrs. McDarnad was talking about numbers. She asked the class if she has twelve apples in one basket, and eight oranges in another basket, how much fruit does she have total? Cameron will never forget the smug, confident look on Alyssa's face when she raised her hand.

Who teaches girls to raise their hands like that anyway?

She raised her hand palm first and then waived it back and forth like a pageant queen. It'd been five years since this day and Cameron still couldn't stand the way that little snotty third grade version of Alyssa raised her hand and said, "You can't compare apples and oranges."

What a birdbrain. I don't know what Isaac sees in her, Cameron thought, with merely a look, almost telepathically to Zoe. Cameron rolled his eyes, and Zoe rolled hers as if they were doing the wave with their eyeballs together.

It's not what he sees in her, it's what he sees on her, Zoe motioned back.

"I can practically hear you two, you know?" Isaac interrupted their silent conversation.

Mr. Docker approached the desk and adjusted the long flexible black microphone cord. Cameron recognized the desk from the auditorium; they used it as a prop in last year's winter play. It was the desk used for Ebenezer Scrooge. Mr. Docker, in his brown tweed sports coat, looked very natural behind the polished wood and granite top desk.

On the other side of the stage, the contestants stood from right to left: Moose, Macie, and Glenda. Moose stroked his bedhead hair and pointed to his buddies in the crowd. Glenda shuffled around highlighted loose-leaf pieces of paper arranging them from opening statement, to most likely asked questions. Macie read and sent texts from her phone and blew kisses to the audience she imagined was paying attention to her.

"Okay students, calm down," Mr. Docker said after the mandatory high-pitched tone of the microphone. "I'm pleased to announce the final candidates for this year's student body presidential race."

Then Mr. Docker said some boring stuff: he explained the school's traditions, rules about how only eighth graders can run, blah, blah, blah, etc., etc., etc.

For a guy whose life's work was producing a morning news show, he doesn't know much about live theater, Isaac noted.

Eventually, Mr. Docker made his way into the debate. Glenda rehearsed her opening statement from memory; they went through a couple softball questions, introductions, all very standard stuff for the first few minutes.

"Now students, here's something interesting," Mr. Docker said, "What's the first change you would make as student body president? Macie, why don't you start?"

"Um, well," Macie started.

Cameron winced. Macie's lips made a smacking sound like her mouth was locked shut, and he could hear all her spit slosh around.

"Like, my first move as student body president would be like making like all the soda machines have more sugar-free options. Like because health, is like one of the most important things for being healthy."

Macie netted hundreds of hours, if not days, standing before a mirror with her cellphone practicing the perfect smile for social media. She stood in front of the microphone and slowly tilted her head to one side, just barely, giving a three-quarter close-lipped smile. That was her whole answer.

"Future doctor," Zoe whispered to Cameron.

"Yeah, but look at that smile," Cameron shook his head. "She's guaranteed 40% of the male vote. Minimum."

"Okay, and what about you, Glenda? Same question." Mr. Docker said.

"After I become student body president . . . " Glenda started.

"Nice assertive line there," Isaac whispered to the two others.

" . . . the first thing I'm going to do, is say thank you to the voters. And I'm going to do that by writing personalized thank you cards to every homeroom teacher's classroom. The thank you note will be handwritten, with every student's name on it. "

Applause.

"In cursive."

More applause.

"But my immediate focus as school president will be replacing the lunch trays in the cafeteria because—" She couldn't finish. The crowd roared in approval. The lunch trays were a constant complaint to any student. They were old, chipped, and faded. They always smelled dirty, and even after coming out of the dishwasher, they seemed to be dusty. It was a simple and well-overdue fix, universally approved.

Glenda didn't say "Hmph" when she looked over to Macie, but anyone who could read minds and/or body language heard it.

"You both hungry or something?" Moose Patrowski interrupted.

Laughter from the audience.

"Okay Moose," Mr. Docker signaled for the crowd to pipe down. "What would your first move be?"

Isaac re-adjusted himself in his seat and crossed his legs. Cameron noticed. *This ought to be interesting,* Cameron thought. *Did he coach his answers too?*

"Um, well Mr. Docker," Moose started.

He was trying to sound intelligent, but the three friends all noticed he started with the same dumb filler word as Macie.

"I'm not sure if you're aware, but a recent state Supreme Court case of *Doe v. District 847,*" Moose read off a notecard.

He continued, "They ruled that it was an unconst—ugh—un-cons-tatu-tion-nal—unconstitutional! They said it was an unconstitutional restriction of the first amendment for a state funded public school to deny a student's right to petition against its uniform policy." He dropped the notecard down and looked at the crowd.

"My first move is going to be getting rid of school uniforms."

Total uproar.

Moose bobbed his head with the cheers, holding high two thumbs up for the crowd. His upraised arms exposed his gut from his un-tucked button-down shirt and sweaty armpits. Cameron and Zoe both shot a raised eyebrow to Isaac.

"Why are you doing this?" Zoe whispered.

"It's your fault," Cameron whispered to Zoe. "I'll explain later."

"I thought this would be a little harder," Isaac shrugged.

CH 07

As Isaac planned, he broke the headline news to the school the next morning that in fact, Moose Patrowski was correct about the uniform thing. *Doe v. District 847* was a real court case in the state. The court confirmed that a public school could not deny its students the right to petition for a removal of school uniforms.

Now, what Isaac didn't get into—likely because it was too complicated to understand the distinction—was the court said the school couldn't deny the students from creating the petition. The court didn't say the school had to grant the petition. But even if Isaac did understand the distinction, he wasn't going to report that on the morning news; that would be bad news. All that mattered was Moose received a huge boost in student support at the mere possibility of getting rid of the uniforms. In reality, this was nothing more than an empty political promise to spark debate.

But that wasn't the most breaking news of the day.

"Alyssa Sonoma has a boyfriend," the Godzilla-sized Cameron Chen loomed over the ant that was Isaac Budgies. In slow motion, the giant Cameron released the bomb he held between two fingers, and Isaac looking up like a cartoon, watched the metaphorical object crash down unto his head, exploding his entire imagined city.

Cameron waited to deliver the news until after school, while they rode their bikes home. He once heard that the best time to talk to one's parents about reproduction was in the car, because it allowed both parties to naturally avoid eye contact. Cameron thought this would be an equally awkward conversation, and figured riding bikes was as close to simulating a car ride as possible.

Isaac slammed on his brakes and turned around to stare at Cameron directly in the face, "How do you know that?"

"Zoe heard her mention it in the locker room during gym," Cameron made an attempt to get back in motion on the bike. *Do not stop moving*, he told himself.

"Wait up," Isaac chased after him. "That's all she got? Give me the W's, man. Who is it? When did it happen? How long have they been dating? Why does she like him? Who. The. Hell. Is. It?"

"Actually, which boggles my mind, it is in fact some high school guy. He's a freshman at Pine Lakes High School," Cameron kept pedaling.

"See, dude? Zoe was right!"

"It still makes no sense to me. Somehow this makes her more popular to other eighth grade girls now?"

"Yes, somehow. I don't know how, or why. But yes. That's exactly what Zoe said would happen. Can we talk for one second about how lame it is for a high school guy to go out with someone in junior high?"

"Agreed."

"I mean, we're not even a month into the school year and this guy's already solidified himself as such an outcast that he's exhausted his well of options in the entire high school?"

Cameron knows if he waited for just a half second, Isaac would probably continue.

"That is so lame, how can Alyssa not know that any freshman in high school who is actively seeking out an eighth grader to start dating is obviously not cool?"

Cameron couldn't resist, "Are you saying you're actually surprised Alyssa doesn't know something?"

"I know you don't like her, Cam, you've made your point, but come on. You agree with me, right? I mean, I guess maybe if they were dating last year and they didn't break-up that's one thing. But once you get to high school there's a barrier. He's crossing the barrier."

Isaac was so fired up he peddled passed Cameron, pumping his legs subconsciously in anger.

"If you think it's so lame, why do you want to date a girl who doesn't know that? Can't you see how contradictory you sound?"

"You can't *see* sound, Chen."

"Why would you want to date a girl who wants to date a high schooler?"

"You don't get it. It's like Zoe told us, it's not lame for Alyssa. Don't you think it would be cool if I was dating a high school girl?"

Cameron smirked; point taken.

"Well, if she's already dating a high schooler, I guess we don't need Moose to win the election anymore, right?" Cameron asked.

Sssshwwwp!

Isaac slammed on the brakes and slid his rear tire in a 180-degree turn and faced Cameron, making an impressive skid track while he did it.

"Just the opposite," Isaac blurted out. "It makes perfect sense. How did I not see this?"

Cameron stopped to check his watch. They still needed to do their homework and put the finishing polish on tomorrow's news script. Cameron didn't have time for Isaac's fantasy dating life. "Go on," he twirled his wrist.

"Alyssa thinks Macie is going to win the election," Isaac clapped.

"Isaac, I am not an 8th grade girl, and I do not possess the narcissism to pretend I understand how to think like one, so you need to spell this out for me. Please."

"Alyssa thinks Macie will win the election. So she went out and found a boyfriend in high school, just like Zoe said she'd do. It makes perfect sense. It's not like she's marrying the guy. It's a popularity stunt. But if Macie loses, she wont need him, she'll still have the morning news to hang over Macie's head."

"You know in a very demented and juvenile manner, I actually get it. What I will never get is how you're into a girl who is clearly insane."

"We need Moose to win. Well, we need Macie to lose."

Cameron shook his head, doubting very much whether Isaac was focused on their broadcasting goals at all. But to show his friend he could follow along, Cameron recited the rest of the plan, "Macie will lose. Then, Alyssa won't have the social pressures of keeping score with Macie. Which means, she won't need a high school boyfriend. She will dump him, and then logically fall in love with you, Isaac Budgies, the man who sits next to her. And you two can fall in love after all?"

Isaac knew when he was being patronized, "Will you at least admit there's no way Glenda Howard, as qualified as she is, could beat Macie on her own?"

"Oh, she'd be screwed," Cameron nodded.

"Which is why we need Moose to win."

"You know what? Maybe you and Alyssa are a good match."

CH 08

"I think we should do a like sit-down type of interview with the candidates," Alyssa suggested to the classroom.

Cameron wanted to groan, but it wasn't actually that bad of an idea. Mr. Docker pinned the idea on the corkboard at the front of the class. The younger students agreed it must be a good idea, because neither Isaac nor Cameron chimed in with a rebuttal.

"I like that, Alyssa," Mr. Docker spoke while he wrote on another notecard to pin to the board. "Go on, what sort of format do we want?"

"Well, I was thinking it would sort of be like a talk show interview, like on Ellen or something. Just one candidate at a time sitting across of me and a coffee table."

Isaac had to put his hands in his pockets to keep from interrupting her. Alyssa had a great idea to do a pre-recorded sit-down, but this isn't the way he'd go about it. Not at all. Ellen was daytime TV, too cozy. A sit down with election candidates should be behind a desk. He tried telling himself to keep calm. Alyssa had her new cry-for-help boyfriend, but she'd likely be friendlier to him now with her boyfriend shield. Isaac wasn't so much of a threat now. He wondered if she knew he knew about her boyfriend.

She has to know I know. Isaac Budgies knows everything; it's my job.

"I like that idea Alyssa," Mr. Docker rubbed his chin. "We'll talk to the theater department and a get a set of those low white seats."

"Yeah, and I think it will be more of a 'Get to Know Them' format," Alyssa said using her fingers to make quotes. "Like more casual questions, favorite movie, stuff like that."

"Okay!" Isaac couldn't resist.

He held his hand straight in the air. He hated this idea. Well, it was a good idea to do a pre-recorded segment—but that was all—he hated everything else about it. "Look, we get these guys sitting down in a room, why not have them at a desk, like a sports panel?"

"Yeah," the students started to agree.

Once again, Alyssa thought to herself. *Why does this guy constantly need to keep showing me up? Just one time let me have an idea, Isaac Budgies!* Alyssa screamed at the top of her lungs, slightly in her head.

The class interjected with further agreement. Mr. Docker pivoted, and before she knew it, Alyssa became a co-anchor to a pre-recorded panel segment with Isaac. After the bell sounded, the classroom cleared out. No one left the room faster than Alyssa. Isaac sprinted after her.

"Hey Alyssa, this is a great idea," Isaac speed-walked, knowing he actually needed to go in the opposite direction to his science class.

"Are you talking to me or yourself?" Alyssa couldn't even look at him.

To an eighth grade boy, eighth grade girls are the most intimidating and ferocious creatures on the planet. But boys forget these merciless creatures have feelings too, and occasionally are capable of vulnerability.

"What do you mean?" He asked.

Inside Isaac's mind, he sat in a military uniform at the control center of a submarine panicking while red lights and sirens alarmed around him. Pressure valves burst with steam and water spilled out of various locations. Inside his mind, he shouted "Mayday!" to anyone that listened through a loudspeaker.

"I think this will be really fun doing a segment together."

While that went on in Isaac's mind, Alyssa envisioned herself sitting before a movie star's make-up mirror. *Sonoma* was written in white letters on the back of her black chair. Little round lights boarded the mirror, and an assistant applied powder to Alyssa's face while another curled her dark brown hair.

"We're ready for you, Ms. Sonoma," the director and her clipboard whispered to her.

Alyssa waved away the assistant and walked through the crowded narrow back hall of the theater, passed wardrobe and onto the main stage. The stage itself was empty, the theater, completely black, with only Isaac Budgies sitting right smack in the middle as her imaginary audience. She approached the center of the stage, standing with her feet shoulder width apart. She took a deep breath, wiggled her toes a little, and exhaled. The singular spotlight clicked on directly over Alyssa. She even envisioned the little dust mites fluttering through the otherwise dark auditorium.

Back in reality, in the halls of Pine Lakes Academy, "You like hijacked my entire idea!" Alyssa turned to face Isaac. Her eyes ever so slightly began to water.

Inside the submarine of Isaac's imagination, the sonar screen bleeped red: "Warning! Warning!" A computerized voice called from the electronic dashboard, speaking over the alarm sirens and clamoring men in the background.

"She's gonna blow!" Isaac hurled into the microphone. He smashed the emergency glass and pounded the *Stop Talking* button, but it was too late.

"Whoa, calm down," Isaac whispered; people were already beginning to stare. In his vanity, he flashed a smile and a wave to a few of the onlooking sixth graders. Fans.

"Don't tell me to calm down!" Alyssa started to cry. Not too much, but she did manage to get a few tears. Last night, with a similar performance for her parents, she wasn't able to cry for some reason. She was glad they came back today. She knew this wasn't actually an issue worth crying over, but that's never stopped her in the past.

"Shhh," Isaac motioned with his outraised hands, "Alyssa, what's the matter?"

"Like, I just like wanted to do this by myself and you ruined it," she exhaled through her nose, somehow finding the strength to collect herself. "Like, I'm not your sidekick!"

"Hey sorry, I wanted to work together on something with you."

"Like, how can you even say this was like my idea?" Alyssa pictured herself walking across the stage, while the spotlight followed her. "I wanted to do like a talk-show panel, and I wanted it to be like me by myself and you stole it from me."

Meanwhile in Isaac's submarine, incoming torpedoes on the sonar approached from straight ahead.

"Fix this, man!" The Captain barked in a Scottish accent to Isaac. "If you can't steer us clear, we're all doomed!"

Isaac wiped the sweat from his brow and used all his might to maneuver the giant ship out of the incoming torpedo's path.

"Okay, okay," Isaac hushed, "We'll lose the desk. We can do the casual thing."

The torpedo just nicked the tail-end of the sub, it made a thunderous clank, but wasn't a direct hit.

"I think you and I can make a really good team," Isaac added as carefully as he would place a Jenga block on to the top of the tower.

"I think we should sit on opposite sides of the panel."

BOOM!

The torpedo exploded outside of range of the sub, but its blast rocked everyone aboard the ship, knocking Isaac to the ground from his control panel.

"Yeah. Sure, we can try that," Isaac spoke to her shoes. "I just thought this could be—"

"Why did you like have totally ambush my idea?" Alyssa sniffled.

She glared at him through her watered eyes. Alyssa did her best to keep the tears balanced on her lids, wanting to see if she could slide one off from each side alternatively.

"I thought it would be fun to work with you," he said it, but the bell rang right when the words came out of his mouth. Embarrassed for admitting it, whether she heard him or not, he couldn't say it again.

"Aaaaand cut!" the director applauded Alyssa from the stage.

"Looks like you're late," she said to Isaac, suddenly without any sign of emotional turmoil whatsoever.

Inside Isaac's imaginary submarine, he collected himself from the ground and stood in about an inch of water. The captain came over to console him.

"You did the best you could," the captain said.

"Are we hit?" Isaac asked.

"We've taken water, but we'll manage. Be careful out there."

CH 09

"This blows," Moose muttered under his breath, "I didn't sign up for spending after school time recording skits."

"Come on, Moose," Isaac spoke out of the side of his mouth, "If you want to be the most powerful popular student in the school, you have to win the election first."

Cameron continued to set up the cameras, but said nothing. Although he agreed to be onboard with helping Moose win the election, he did not agree to like the idea or to not complain about it. *Moose,* Cameron thought to himself, *is a dumbass.*

Cameron really let him have it too when Isaac admitted to caving into Alyssa's idea. Cameron assumed immediately that Alyssa probably started crying and that's when Isaac caved, but Isaac said it wasn't the reason. Isaac said he was going to change his mind before she started crying.

Isaac and Moose moved the chairs around the auditorium stage. Isaac still hated the idea of doing a casual daytime TV show format. Yet, if he was going to do it, he at least wanted to show up first and arrange the furniture. Moose arrived early because Isaac purposely told him the start time was 20 minutes earlier than the actual time. Technically, Moose arrived 15 minutes late. It was Cameron's idea to tell him the wrong time, but Isaac was sure he would have thought of it too.

Just like a lawyer prepping a witness before taking the stand, Isaac wanted to run through some key points with Moose. Moose hoped the sooner they started the sooner they'd be done and he could get home and play video games.

"Alyssa is going to grill him," Cameron whispered to Zoe by shaking his head and checking his watch. Cameron and Zoe worked mostly in silence while focusing on focusing the cameras to where the chairs would be.

"I'm taking away uniforms, I'm going to win," Moose reminded Isaac.

"Well, Macie jumped on board with that, so now it's still going to be a tight race."

"She can't do that, I said it first!"

"Moose, anyone can say whatever they want. You can't call dibs on a policy platform. These are things a school president needs to know."

"Hey man, you're the one who wants me to run."

"Are you saying you don't want to do this?" Isaac rebutted. "Does big shot Moose Patrowski want to lose?"

Moose recoiled. As the star of the eighth grade basketball team, also winning school president would be one of the coolest things he could possibly do. Moose didn't need much to be persuaded to win anything, especially a contest. The thought that Moose would be the king of the school if he won the election made the decision a no-brainer. What Moose didn't think much about was the responsibility that came with the title.

"No, I do. I'm just saying let's hurry it up, that's all."

"There he is," Isaac smiled. "Now remember, I'm here for your own good. I'm sure Alyssa and Macie prepped all these questions together. This whole thing is a ploy to give Macie an advantage."

"You're here for me, and Alyssa's prepping Macie; who's going to help Glenda?"

"Trust me, Moose, you need all the help you can get. Don't worry about Glenda, she knows what she's doing."

"Oh hey, Isaac," Glenda waived.

Glenda walk in with a single book held tightly to her chest, smile as wide as the Grand Canyon.

Gosh, can people actually be this nice? Cameron wondered. He was also annoyed she showed up early.

Isaac could have used a few more minutes of prep time with his puppet.

Isaac greeted Glenda, and perhaps he would have said more, but Alyssa followed shortly behind. Isaac's attention for Glenda lapsed. Surprisingly, Alyssa entered without Macie. She came in prepared with notecards, almost professional.

Don't jump up so eager like that, dude, Zoe said to herself noting Isaac's immediate change in countenance and behavior when Alyssa entered the room.

Zoe noticed how Cameron's best friend, and self-proclaimed mastermind of the universe turned to putty at the sight of Alyssa. Isaac could probably find a girlfriend fairly easily if he wanted one, but he only wanted Alyssa—this month—and she certainly doesn't want anything to do with him.

And he turns into a complete sap around her. It's getting worse too. I think he's beginning to like her more. But why? Because she wants nothing to do with him, that's why. Boys are dumb.

Zoe wondered which happened first: Alyssa's rejection of Isaac or Isaac's crush on Alyssa. Zoe assumed the rejection came first, which led to the crush. But she knew Isaac pretty well, and the very first thing was that push-up bra.

"I brought this book because I thought it would make a nice little center piece on the coffee table," Glenda offered.

Cameron noticed she decided not to say hello to Alyssa. *So, maybe she's not so nice after all. I liker her.*

I hate her, Alyssa said to herself. Unaware that she didn't say hello to Glenda either. But in her mind, someone like Glenda should say hello to her first.

Macie walked in last. She very obviously spent the last half hour in the bathroom applying, removing, and reapplying make-up. Her cheeks reflected most of the lights in the room, and her eyelids were a smear of all the color options in her make-up kit.

Zoe groaned at Macie's grand entrance. *Who teaches a young girl to put make-up on like this?*

Alyssa applied a liberal amount of dark shadow on the tops of her eyes, caked herself in glitter, and slapped on about 10 coats of lipstick. If she wore a wig, one would think she dressed up for Halloween.

Her mother must be very unintelligent allowing her daughter to wear make-up like that. My mom would never let me dress like that, Zoe thought. *She looks like a backup dancer in a music video. Who actually thinks this looks attractive?*

Moose hadn't blinked since Macie walked in. He fixated on her like a moth to a patio light. *Right*, Zoe shrugged, *dumb guys.*

Isaac, momentarily forgetting that he wanted Alyssa to like him, instinctively took to center stage when the last guest arrived.

"Okay everyone, thanks for coming today—"

Oh no he doesn't! Alyssa said to herself. *This is MY project. MY taping.*

She leapt to Isaac's side, and interrupted him. "—Okay, like, as you all know, I like wanted to give you all like one last opportunity to like showcase yourselves to the school before voting starts next week."

Alyssa won her little prize. They filmed a staged coffee table discussion on a couch, two chairs, and three cameras; one set as a wide shot, and the other two Cameron and Zoe frantically operated themselves to get close ups of each speaker, moving in rotating unison, like synchronized dancers. Cameron planned to spend the entire recording session fretting about how much of a nightmare it will be to edit and splice everything together. Zoe would help. Cameron liked editing videos with Zoe, even though it was a lot of work, it was an enjoyable thing to do, which makes work not feel like working at all. Helping Moose win an election, that was real work.

Cameron zoomed in on Alyssa as she got seated. It's a unique opportunity being able to work a camera like that. Sure, everyone can zoom in on a photo, but a photo is old, it's a memory of a moment gone. Twisting the handle nob with his right hand, like squeezing the throttle on a motorcycle, Cameron zoomed all the way in, so that Alyssa's face filled the frame. To be that close to someone live was kind of like having a super power. Cameron studied her. Her tan skin hid behind red blush; make-up smothered her eyelashes, eyebrows, nose line, and lips. Cameron saw for a second something he'd never noticed about Alyssa before: she was nervous. He could see it in the small contractions of her jaw muscle when her smile dropped. She forced it back up like pulling the cords on heavy window blinds. Her dark eyes danced around the room failing to rest on a focus point. Her nostrils flared out.

Cameron zoomed out. He felt guilty, as if he walked in on her changing, or he overheard her telling a secret he wasn't supposed to know. As he panned out for a portrait shot, Alyssa's nerves faded out of focus.

Oh my gosh, I'm so nervous, Alyssa thought to herself manually pinching her nostrils together.

"Okay Cameron," she made eye contact with him through the camera monitor. The way she lowered her eyes to a snarl, made Cameron wonder if she knew what he was up to. "Are you done playing around back there, can we get this moving?"

CH 10

"Greetings, Pine Lakes Academy, I'm Alyssa Sonoma and I'm joined by our three final candidates for this year's Student Body President."

"Cut," Isaac stood up and pointed to the camera.

"Oh come on Isaac," Alyssa groaned.

"Well aren't you going to introduce me?"

"Oh sorry. I guess since I don't think you should be here, I keep forgetting I have to introduce you."

Isaac shrugged off the insult with a smirk and a forced laughed.

"Okay no problem," he waived. "Let's try it one more time. Give me a quick intro and then I'll just lead straight in with a question of who we have here, and you got it."

It irritated Alyssa to the depths of her core. She could never be sure if Isaac knew when she insulted him. She'd never met someone so in love with himself. Was he refusing to take the hint?

Wow, he is such a hunk, Glenda thought to herself. *Oh my gosh! Pull it together, G.*

Glenda dusted off her skirt and readjusted herself in the seat. To the outside observer, she looked normal. Well, normal isn't the right word for a girl like Glenda Howard: back-to-back district science fair champ, mathlete, and straight-A student. She looked like a dork. Glenda needed to calm down. Winning student council president would be great experience before she entered high school, where she'd run for class president. Glenda needed to be class president in high school to help get accepted into an Ivy League college. An Ivy League college would open doors for her first internship, and then from there, a career in politics.

School was just a stepping-stone for girls like Glenda. Glenda's mother always reminds her, "You need prior experience to get more experience."

In about ten years after junior high, when most people go back to look at old yearbook pictures, many will come to Glenda Howard's page and realize she's a very funny and beautiful girl. They'll finally notice hiding behind her big glasses and dark bangs, were bright eyes and high cheekbones. And those former classmates will wonder why they didn't hang out with Glenda more back when they were in junior high.

But, nobody knows that yet, except Glenda. And Glenda knows the reason will have been because in reality, it was Glenda who chose to not hang out with them. She's known all along not to waste her time on things that don't help her goals.

Glenda liked Isaac. Not *like* liked him; she didn't have time for that. Plus, he wasn't Ivy League material. So, she could never marry him, but she liked him. *It's not easy being the greatest news anchor in Pine Lakes Academy's history*, Glenda presumed. Sure, she was aware of the element of vanity required for the job, and how he always did his little catch phrase at the end of each episode. But, he was one of the most ambitious guys at Pine Lakes Academy, and to someone like Glenda, ambition was cool. Ambition was hot.

While Glenda gave herself an internal pep-talk, which fired through her adolescent mind in about two split seconds, she curled her bottom lip to blow her bangs away from her glasses.

"Okay, we're ready to reset," Cameron points to Alyssa, "Whenever you're ready."

"Greetings Pine Lakes Academy, Alyssa Sonoma here, joined by fly-on-the-wall Isaac Budgies and your three Pine Lakes Academy Student Council Presidential candidates."

This is gonna get messy, Zoe thought to herself.

📽️ 📽️ 📽️

"... and cut," Cameron waived down to the five guests in the chairs. He popped his eyes wide, adjusted his glasses, and exhaled puffing his cheeks to Zoe.

Moose slunk down in his chair; Isaac stretched his face with his hands clasped over his mouth. Perhaps Glenda's face told the story best: it looked like she was sucking on a lemon the way she wrestled back a smile.

Zoe cringed towards Cameron and mouthed, "wow" to him in silence.

The taping didn't go well. Actually, it went swimmingly for Glenda who only needed about two minutes to realize she was stuck in a power struggle between Isaac and Alyssa. Alyssa made it very clear early on that she intended to embarrass Moose. Moose made it equally clear, that he was an embarrassing clown. Isaac hadn't prepared himself properly for Moose's level of stupidity. What Zoe and Cameron wondered watching the onslaught was whether Alyssa realized that as much as she was hurting Moose, she actually made Glenda look much better than Macie.

Alyssa asked several questions throughout the interview that proved Moose was not only unfit to be student council president, but it seemed that he didn't even know what that meant. At one point Alyssa asked Moose how he would "balance basketball, wrestling and student council?"

"What do you mean balancing?" Moose asked.

"Well, Moose, student council President is going to take up a lot of your time, you're already very involved with sports, how will you manage to do everything?"

Moose processed the question and it looked as if his brain moved at about the speed of a 30 year-old printer. Finally, he responded, "You mean this isn't just like a contest?"

All the participants on the couch laughed, but from Zoe and Cameron's vantage point behind the camera, they could tell this was no joke. Moose didn't know anything about a student council member's requirements or responsibilities, let alone the president.

Moose went even further to ask, "How many times a week do you think I'll have to stay after school?"

But he didn't ask it like a conversation starter, he said it directly to Isaac, as if they were having a side-bar conversation.

Isaac, the professional fertilizer salesman that he was responded, "Great question, Moose. Macie, what do you think is the appropriate amount of time commitment for a student body president to volunteer?"

During that line of questioning, Glenda wished Isaac would have asked her that question. Her answer would have been, "All the time."

Isaac helped Moose navigate the minefield of his own naïve stupidity, while Macie made Glenda look like the obvious choice. Not to say that Macie was bad. She rehearsed with Alyssa, and knew all the buzz words, but she lacked showmanship. Too scripted, too obvious she practiced. If Macie Neadle was going to win, it would be because she's beautiful, popular, and people wanted her to like them. And she knew it. For Alyssa this was a cut and dry popularity contest. That's why she sat with her dress pulled high and her sweater low.

"So, like can I watch the video?" Macie already replaced the gum in her mouth.

"No, we need to edit this and cut it all together," Zoe replied. "You can watch it along with everyone else tomorrow morning."

"Lots of editing," Isaac reiterated to Cameron.

"Okay, but like, can you send it to me so I can post it?"

"I'll have to ask Mr. Docker tomorrow after it airs," Zoe wished she could just say no, but figured this answer would be less likely to have another response.

"So, this is going on tomorrow morning?" Glenda wondered to Isaac.

"Yeah, you did really good," Isaac said. "You'll see tomorrow.

"Really *well*," she smiled. "See you tomorrow."

Glenda skipped out of the recording session saying goodbye to only Zoe and Isaac. That night, when she got home, Glenda was so giddy from the compliment—albeit grammatically incorrect—she needed to do all the unassigned math questions from the most recent chapter to help her calm down.

Alyssa and Macie walked out together, they didn't say goodbye to anyone.

When the door shut behind them, Moose whispered from his chair, "Alright."

"Alright what?" Isaac asked. "Nothing about that was alright."

"Yeah man, that was terrible," Cameron added, "You know—"

But before Cameron could finish, Moose stood up from his seat, reminding Cameron and Isaac that although he was not as smart as them, he was much bigger.

"Okay, so I maybe blew it just now, okay," Moose said.

Um you think? Zoe asked herself.

"But that chick just tried to make me look like an idiot, and nobody makes Moose Patrowski look dumb."

Except yourself? Zoe wanted to ask.

"This isn't a joke anymore. I'm winning this election. I'll be honest, this after school crap, and all this other junk sounds awful, but I am *not*! going to let her beat me."

"What do you think, Cam?" Isaac asked. "Think we can swing this into a positive?"

"I think Moose, you need to make up your freaking mind," Cameron said. "The whole school is voting in two days. Do you want it or not?"

"Yeah."

"Yeah what?" Cameron dug deeper.

"Yeah I want it."

"What do you want?"

"I want to win student council president," Moose got a little louder.

"You *want* to win or you're *going* to win?"

Cameron always imagined giving a locker room halftime speech. *Is this what sports feels like?* He thought.

"Who are you?" Zoe mumbled to Cameron.

"Yes, I am going to win!" Moose declared.

"What are you going to win?" Cameron shook a fist at Moose. *Sports are fun.*

"I am going to win student council president!" Moose yelled.

The dust of excitement settled through the air, and Cameron blushed to Isaac and Zoe knowing he let himself get carried away.

"Okay then," Cameron said. "Then we found your angle."

"Ah!" Isaac snapped. "Cameron, you're a genius." Isaac said it to compliment Cameron, but of course, it takes a genius to recognize a genius.

Isaac continued, "Moose, you started this whole thing thinking the contest was a joke, right?"

Zoe looked to Cameron for reassurance that Isaac was in fact on the same page as her boyfriend. The way he threw his hand off to one side was a disappointing sign that, yes, Isaac was taking the words out of his mouth.

"This whole thing was a joke to you, and if Cam and Zoe here can work any miracles on this editing, then perhaps we can pull off some of your dumbass answers as jokes. You have to play the class clown."

Moose scratched his head, "You can do that?"

"I can edit anything into a comedy," Zoe said. "Even a documentary on cloning. It's just about how you splice it."

"Nothing for that one?" Zoe asked.

"It was okay," Isaac shrugged.

"I don't get," Moose said.

"Just keep the kids laughing for two more days and you win," Cameron said.

"You can do it," Zoe said with a sarcastic fist pump and chipper voice.

"I'm going to be student council president," Moose smiled.

"And it was all my idea," Isaac boasted.

"You're both idiots," said Cameron.

"The whole school is screwed," Zoe moaned. "And I feel like it's my fault."

"Oh this is totally your fault," Cameron said.

"Definitely," Isaac agreed.

CH 11

Moose's competitive spirit finally caught election fever. He no longer felt like Isaac's pawn. *I'm doing this for me*, Moose convinced himself.

That morning, Moose rolled out of bed in the t-shirt and jeans he wore the night before, he looked himself in the mirror. His red hair sprang out from his head in all directions, and puffing his bottom jaw forward, he sniffed the foulness of his own morning breath.

"Ladies and Gentleman!" Moose shouted to the bathroom mirror. He held his toothbrush as a microphone, "Tipping the scales at two hundred pounds, standing six foot one inches tall," then Moose pounded on his chest. "Pine Lakes Academy's all time leading point scorer, voted back to back by the sixth and seventh grade girls as third-cutest boy in class—but shoulda been first place—the *baaadest*, the *meeaaanst*, the *hhaawwtteest!* Man. Alive. And Your. New! Student.

Council. Pressssideeent! The Marvelous, the Magnificent, Moose Paaattrooowwskiiii!"

Moose nodded at the mirror with pride. Then he threw the toothbrush back in its holster, indifferent as to whether he remembered if actually brushed his teeth. *Time for school.*

📷 📷 📷

Moose strutted into school wearing a fake mustache, aviator sunglasses, and a tie-dyed school sweatshirt printed with a picture of him wearing the same outfit on the front. Across the top and bottom of the sweatshirt in big bold letters, it read, "Can't Lose with Moose."

"Let's win this thing," he said to Isaac and Cameron at the entrance of the school.

Isaac snapped a picture with his phone, planning on running it as part of the morning's announcement. The voter polls opened in 24-hours.

📷 📷 📷

Later that morning, in the Advanced Pine Lakes Academy News class, Mr. Docker wanted to start getting cameras on location to plan for the next two days. Thanks to the meddling of Isaac Budgies, all signs indicated this would be the hottest contested election of all time. But of course, even if it were not for Isaac Budgies, Mr. Docker still planned on running the headline "Most Heated Election of All Time!" He always used a variant of this every year.

"I don't see what the big deal is for us," Jenny Towlel, the seventh grade weather person said. "I mean, like, why are we focusing so much on just the election? There's other stuff we could be talking about too, right?"

"Other 'stuff'?" Cameron leaned over his desk in protest. "We jumped nearly two full percentage points in the sixth grade viewership since we started covering the election."

"Dude, the McLennan family transferred to school last week; they have triplets," Zoe rolled her eyes.

"I'm going off the data," Cameron exclaimed.

"I'm just saying, I think we could be doing some more student interest pieces," Jenny Towlel stood her ground.

Unfortunately, she stood on a transparent platform of self-promotion. Sure, if Mr. Docker decided to run with a two-minute on-location segment detailing some up and coming student bands, who better to report on such a thing than Jenny herself? But, one must respect the tenacity.

"No, for the rest of the week, we're on election," Mr. Docker confirmed. "Jenny, you'll have plenty of time for that all year, but election is the big story right now. We need to beat this to the ground until it's over or something else big and shiny and new comes in. Okay?"

"Okay," Jenny pouted.

"We need to get some footage of students at the polls," Mr. Docker said.

"I'd like to have all of the contestants in the room when the results are announced," Isaac interrupted.

Mr. Docker paused and made a mental note, *Every once in a while, this pain in my neck has a good idea.*

Isaac gave a quick glance at Jenny. This was a teaching opportunity: The proper way to pitch an idea, is first having a good idea.

"We have natural tension in the room," Isaac continued. "And we'll cover the spectrum of emotions between the winner and losers. It'll be great."

And that's why I hate this guy, Alyssa said to herself. *Gosh, would he literally like die if someone else came up with an idea?* But she also felt a bit of concern; Alyssa saw the shared glance between Isaac and Jenny. *Is Isaac moving on? Like two days ago, he was like practically drooling over me during the interview. The guy like couldn't even get through a sentence without mumbling over himself. Did I like turn him away? Ugh, Boys.*

Mr. Docker called on an unnamed and unimportant sixth grade boy raising his hand in the back of the room. After the whole class turned to look at him, the boy asked, "We all pretty much agree that this election is a done deal though, right? Like, obviously Moose Patrowski wins?"

It didn't surprise Isaac only a very few "No's" came in response to the boy's question. Alyssa Sonoma's voice belonged to one of them. But what blew him away was that he also heard a "No" coming from Mr. Docker.

"Well who do *you* think wins?" Isaac asked the teacher.

"Listen, I've been around this school long enough to know that it's not really a done deal until the votes are in."

Mr. Docker responded, in what Zoe correctly identified as a classic backtrack. This non-answer suggested he thinks Glenda would win, or at least that's what Zoe thought he was thinking.

"Why are you so sure Moose is going to win?" Alyssa asked Isaac, gyrating her neck with every syllable. "Other than the fact you like basically told the whole school to vote for him."

It's now or never. Jenny Towlel decided to herself. *You want to play hardball with the big girls? Then you need to be aggressive. B-e aggressive.*

"It's either going to be Moose or Glenda," Jenny responded on Isaac's behalf. An act of total defiance, as it was no secret Alyssa supported Macie. *That's right*

Alyssa; I'm going to be the next news anchor. So, watch out!

Girls don't just accidentally fall into the "popular" clique; it's earned by being mean and calculated. Alyssa didn't even flinch at the comment. She showed absolutely zero response to Jenny. Her eyes stayed locked on Isaac, and she continued to Isaac, "You're done pulling strings." And she wiggled her fingers like a puppeteer while she said it. "You don't always get what you want."

Jenny sat in the back wondering if the words even came out of her mouth. She was sure she spoke them out loud. She fought the urge of putting her hand to her throat like the Little Mermaid. This was definitely a move she'd remember and something she already couldn't wait to have the opportunity to use next year. A complete one hundred percent ignore. *Touché, Alyssa. And goodbye to anyone letting me get a say in this argument.*

"Alyssa, the second Moose threw his hat in the ring Macie became the long shot," Zoe jumped in for support of Isaac. She too ignored Jenny completely, but not because Zoe was being rude, but because just actually wasn't paying attention until just then.

To hear Macie being labeled a long shot was actually music to Alyssa's ears. She'd want nothing more than to be able to show she did *everything* she could to help her best frenemy win a popularity contest. *But oh if she were to lose!* That would be a huge blow to Macie's colossal ego. Alyssa had the chance to seize ultimate control of the "most popular girl in school" title. Plus, word about her high school boyfriend was spreading quickly. *Should be.* She laughed to herself. *I was practically screaming about it in the locker room.*

But none of this changed the complicated fact that Alyssa didn't want the weasel Isaac to hold a victory over her head. Alyssa hated Isaac, but she also sort of hated Macie, yet pretended to be Macie's friend. So now Alyssa wasn't so sure whether she wanted Macie to lose the election or see Isaac's candidate lose. This was getting too complex for her, and she hated math. *That's it. I'm voting for Glenda,* Alyssa decided. *She's like literally the best choice anyway.*

CH 12

Pine Lakes Academy worked hard to make the election *feel* like it was an important day. Propaganda supporting either Macie, Glenda, or Moose shouted from every adhesive friendly wall for two weeks. Teachers, who couldn't help but get involved made *#vote* posters to fill any remaining empty space. According to Zoe, the whole scene invoked a sense of extremist nationalism. Especially the *#vote* posters; they seemed very unnecessary since voting was mandatory.

"It's not like we're out here exercising our first amendment rights," Zoe continued to Cameron. The two worked quickly to set up a camera to go around the sixth grade homeroom classes during the vote. "If anything, isn't a mandatory vote some kind of violation of our rights?"

"Who knows?" Cameron's black hair stood extra straight today; he had a lot to coordinate. "Most of these signs are self-serving."

"How so?"

"Those teacher signs aren't for us; they're for Ms. Ferris—or whichever other attention grabber made them—to post on their social media page."

"Hmm. I did see Ms. Ferris taking a selfie out here actually," Zoe admitted.

"Yeah see? The signs aren't for us. They're for our teachers' online presence."

"What did teachers do before social media?" Zoe wondered.

"Teach."

🎥 🎥 🎥

Meanwhile, Mr. Docker paired up Isaac and Alyssa to cover some of the seventh grade homerooms. Isaac struggled to find something to say while walking down the halls alone with Alyssa. She kept her eyes on her phone.

Come on, man. Isaac said to himself. *Imagine if this was just any other person, someone normal, I wouldn't be embarrassed.* Isaac imagined how he'd act if paired with anyone else to capture footage. He'd be talking and making jokes all the way down the corridor. But with Alyssa, he had nothing. *Pretend it's Jenny.* But this didn't work either.

"What?" Isaac asked her, hearing just the faintest sound coming from her mouth.

"Didn't say anything," Alyssa didn't look up from her phone.

In a split second, inside Isaac's mind, he transferred into a police surveillance van. Three different versions of himself hunched over with headphones, mustaches, and cups of coffee sat in the van. The wall of the van displayed several black and white security camera angles of Isaac and Alyssa walking down the hallway, with other monitors keeping track of the sound and volume.

"Ohh" One of the stake-out versions of Isaac said to the other. "Not a great start."

"Run the tape back. What was her exact reply?" another Isaac asked.

"Didn't say anything."

"But did she say 'didn't say anything' or did she say 'I didn't say anything'?"

"What's da difference?" the last cop said. He spoke with a New York sounding accent. "She don't wanna talk to him."

Back in reality, Isaac panicked.

"You ever work one of these portable cameras before?"

"No."

Back in the van inside Isaac's mind: "This guy is taking a beating!"

"Kind of weird Docker would pair us up together, right?" the real Isaac asked. *If she doesn't answer to this then I'm not saying anything else.*

"Why do you say that?"

The surveillance team all jumped from their seats to huddle around one of the headsets so they could all listen in. They replayed the tape, and confirmed. *She asked a question!*

"This is officially a conversation," one of the fake Isaac stakeout officers said.

"I'm just saying, why would he put the two star anchors both on one camera team? You'd think he'd probably want someone else here to hold the camera, right?"

"Well, seems simple enough to me. Only one of us knows how to use the camera."

"Oh come on. We'll switch off. All you gotta do is hit this red button really."

"Don't belittle me," she snapped.

The surveillance team noted the sound monitoring needle spike when she yelled.

"Wow, what? I'm just saying it's not that hard to—why do you give me such a hard time?" Isaac changed lanes.

"Cause your always trying to steal my spotlight," she replied in a near whisper. Scared to death they'd have an argument in a hallway, like a real couple ... again.

"I'm trying to share it," Isaac explained, he reached his hand out metaphorically offering both an olive branch, and his heart.

"I have a boyfriend," she went back to looking at her phone, ending the conversation.

The troopers in the van all jumped back from the audio. "He's dying in there," one of them said. Then into the mic, which connected to Isaac's imaginary earpiece, "Get out of there. I repeat: get out of there."

"Wait, what do you mean? That's not what I meant," Isaac clarified.

Alyssa didn't reply.

"Alright, pack it up boys," the surveillance guy said. "Nothing to see here."

They walked in silence until they reached the first classroom.

Cameron and Zoe, Isaac and Alyssa, and one other pair of students with portable cameras strolled the school grabbing footage of Voting Day. Mr. Docker instructed them to get not only interviews, but if possible, action shots of the students voting. PLAN was going to air a special afternoon broadcast of the results.

The two other teams had no issues getting their footage. Isaac and Alyssa spent a lot of time debating who would hold the camera. Alyssa realized if she just acted a little nicer or even flirted a little while they walked down the hallway, Isaac would have been more agreeable to only holding the camera, maybe. But she snapped at him early, and now he wasn't giving any ground. Eventually, Isaac conceded that Alyssa could capture all but one of the sixth grade homerooms.

Isaac thought Alyssa was texting on her phone during their walk, but she was actually preparing her on-camera introduction. Isaac was impressed by her dedication.

"Don't you think about what you want to say before you go on camera?" Alyssa asked.

Isaac shook his head; "I'm not too big on the whole think before you speak philosophy."

"Exhibit A," she replied.

"But, thinking *while* I speak, that's more my style."

"I'm ignoring you again," she wiped her hair so that it flew over one shoulder, and behind the other. "Let's get this camera set up and rolling. I'll go first."

They walked into the first seventh grade room, and to Isaac's surprise, Alyssa gave an actually flawless introduction and explanation of the days' events. *Can't wait until Chen hears that one. See? She's kinda smart.* Isaac panned across the teacher's desk and zoomed in on the stack of voting scantron sheets yet to be distributed.

"Not bad," Isaac complimented her lowering the camera.

"It's not my first rodeo," she winked, regretting it instantly. *Don't flirt now, what's the point?* "Okay, let's keep it moving."

When it was Isaac's turn to get in front of the camera, he tried not to be condescending to Alyssa while explaining that the "REC" in the bottom corner of the display confirmed when she was in fact recording.

"I think I can manage," she locked a half-smile at the same time as slightly tweaking her neck.

However, Alyssa actually never recorded before.

I'll show this cocky jerk, she thought to herself. Instantly, Alyssa transformed into an Avant-grad cinematographer. She wide framed on the distribution of the vote sheets. The wide shot signaling the broad sweeping impact of the vote. Then, she tight-zoomed on a frame of a random sixth grade girl, signifying the intimacy of voting and it's student-by-student impact. When it was time to interview Isaac, she held the camera so that his head was the exact midpoint of the screen, symbolizing his own self-centeredness. Alyssa couldn't wait to review the footage, she was almost as excited to see her camera work behind the camera as she was to see herself in front of it, but only almost. *Because let's be serious, it's not like camera operators win Oscars*, she reasoned.

"We're getting a live look-in into Mrs. Bescomb's sixth grade class placing their votes. Lots to consider as a 6th grader here. Do you go with the popular vote, which would have to be Macie Neadle, or do you take a more practical candidate, like Glenda Howard? We've heard her promise a better field trip schedule and more privileges to the higher grades. Finally, they could go with Moose Patrowski, the most exciting candidate, who may or may not be back for reelection next year. Moose was the originator of the banning of the school uniform platform, which was soon adopted by Macie as well. Lots and lots to consider here, we'll find out soon."

With a wink, Isaac signed off. He made a quick sharp slash of his hand across his neck to signal to stop recording.

It's the subtleties of Isaac that Alyssa hated most. *Urgh!* She screamed to herself. *Did I really need that queue? Does he think I'm not capable of knowing when to cut off a freaking feed? I've been doing this for three freaking years!* But Alyssa didn't say any of that, she smiled and put the camera down.

"See? Now there's a smile," Isaac clapped at Alyssa.

The comment annoyed her so much she forgot to stop recording. Alyssa casually let the camera flop with her wrist while she stuck her neck out at Isaac. She didn't say anything but continued to stare at him, communicating they were not on friendly terms. Mrs. Bescomb collected the scantron papers from the students around the room and took them to her desk.

"Moose is going to win," one of the sixth grade boys yelled out the second Mrs. Bescomb took his scantron away.

"Duh," another boy agreed, "Who wouldn't vote for the team captain?"

Isaac noticed several girls exchanging quick nodes of approval; Alyssa saw it too. Apparently, Moose had better numbers with the young female electorate than anticipated. An added bonus Isaac and Cameron overlooked. Surely, Moose would get nearly every vote from Mrs. Bescomb's sixth grade class. As the newscasters walked out of the room, Mrs. Bescomb placed the scantrons inside a manila envelope and sealed it shut. She'd hand deliver the votes herself.

CH 13

Ms. Lungar oversaw all student council activities. She was a youngish—about 30-something—slender, tall and curly-haired. She often wore knee-length pencil skirts and medium height heels. Ms. Lungar was quite possibly the most powerful person in her own little world, and the most talented. She was a loudmouthed busybody.

Principal Edwin Wallney wouldn't have it any other way. The old grizzled man kept a countdown calendar at this desk to retirement: 713 days. That's the rest of this school, and one final year next year. Then he's riding off into the sunset and "So long disobedient students," "bon voyage teacher complaints," "adios administrative problems," and "see you in hell you badgering, relentless, tormenting parents!"

Assistant Principal Lungar was a godsend for Principal Wallney. She had aspiration, which is good, but she was also dumb and self-absorbed, which was perfect. Wallney had been around too long to know he didn't need to worry about being fired. So, when Lungar stomped into his office wanting to take the reigns, he gladly handed them over. Wallney hadn't done a single day's worth of real work in over two years. In fact, most students at the school thought that Ms. Lungar was the principal. That meant those students' parents called her instead of him. She was the best.

So naturally, when Ms. Lungar told Mr. Wallney she planned on taking over the student council administration, Wallney fed her the same slop he'd been serving up for the last two years, "Are you sure there's not too much on your plate?"

A normal person might have caught on to the undertone cynicism in a comment like that after the 20th or 30th time hearing it, but not Ms. Lungar. She was so power-hungry; if it sounded like a compliment, she gobbled it up.

"Absolutely not, Principal Wallney," she smiled, "I think it would be good for the school's executive branch to have a more controlling hand in the student legislature."

Mr. Wallney, paused to mull over the thought for awhile. The thought being whether he wanted to order pepperoni or bacon pizza for lunch. Then, he said, "Well, if you think you can handle it, I don't think there's anyone better for the job."

And that's how Ms. Lungar became faculty overseer of the student council.

🎥 🎥 🎥

Ms. Lungar sat in her office with Moose, Macie, and Glenda.

"I want to first congratulate all three of you," she said. "I know how hard it is to run a political campaign."

[Deleted scene of 10 minutes of boring dialog from an anecdotal story told by Ms. Lungar, about the time she ran for student body president as a eighth grader at Pine Lakes Academy. (She lost to a popular girl, very similar to Macie, but left this out of the monolog).]

[An additional deletion here, as she goes on to say how that initial loss didn't stop her gumption. For another few minutes she discussed her illustrious campaigning career as a student council member in high school, and college. Ms. Lungar further sidetracked because she went to college out of state, and that as only eighth graders, the three of them wouldn't understand some of the difficulties of moving away from home for the first time. Finally, a few more minutes on how terrible Ms. Lungar's freshman college roommate was. Ms. Lungar not so subtly hinted at the fact that her roommate was similar to Macie.]

"Anyways, where was I? I didn't realize you students would have so many questions, we've gone on quite a tangent," Ms. Lungar placed her long fingers on her sternum but kept her palm pitched up like a tent. "I wanted to let you know, that regardless of who wins, I want to invite the other two los—uh—the other two non-winners, to act as committee chairs. I have several, several committees in mind. And don't worry, they'd alternate days, so you won't have to fret about conflicting morning meetings."

Moose raised his index finger the air, "One second. Did you say 'morning' meetings?"

"Well yes, of course, when else do you think student council meets?"

"He probably doesn't know," Glenda Howard raised both eyebrows at him.

"No. I mean, like I know student council meets. I wasn't sure about like in the morning," Moose squirmed in his seat. "It's not like it's everyday."

"Is that a question?" Glenda prodded.

"Well, it's probably not more than once a year, obviously right? I'd guess."

Ms. Lungar howled a laugh and fixed her hair, "Moose, you are hilarious. I only plan on having two full representative meetings a week, plus a focus group. That would give you at least two mornings a week to run a side committee."

"If he wins," Alyssa added.

"At least three a week huh?" Moose gulped, "In the mornings? What time do these meetings start?"

"Oh, I don't think they need to be much more than an hour, but that's something I'd want to discuss with the class representatives."

Glenda took notes. She agreed with everything Ms. Lungar said. She could use a few more activities in the morning. "You know, I always thought once a week meetings were never enough."

Macie didn't care. For her, this was about being the most popular girl in school. Nothing else mattered. *Sure, schedule the meetings*, she thought to herself. Didn't matter to her. With a class president win, there was no way anyone could take her off the throne, high school boyfriend or not. *President? More like Queen*, she smiled, completely zoned out from the conversation. *I like the sound of Queen.*

Moose wiped the sweat off his forehead exiting Ms. Lungar's office. *I can't do this. I can't do this. I don't want to deal with this nerd crap. Why am I doing this?* Moose worried himself, turning the corner into the school's main hallway. Moose was so focused on worrying about winning that he didn't see the troop of seventh grade girls in the hallway. He barged right into them.

"Hey, Moose," Jenny Towlel smiled. "Watch where you're going, Mr. President."

"Oh hey, sorry," Moose smiled.

"We were all just talking about how cool it will be when you win," one of the others said, twirling her hair.

The comment might as well have been an allergy pen injection of pure confidence. The cold surge of pride flooded through Moose's veins. "You think so?"

"Moose. Like are you kidding me? Do you even know how totally crazy it would be for you to beat Macie Needle?"

"Yeah," another one said. "She's like, literally the most popular girl in school."

"But if you win," Jenny gave a soft hit to Moose's arm, "That means you're even cooler than she is."

"Don't forget about us when you're the hottest guy in school," another one said.

"Oh come one girls, you know. I'm like the most humble guy in school," Moose bragged.

"That's why we voted for you."

Moose backed away from the conversation and headed to the broadcast room to prepare for the results. *Oh yeah,* Moose reminded himself, *that's why I signed up for this.*

CH 14

"Zoe, how much time do you need to strip this election footage and make a montage? We want to start with a musical intro of all the students voting," Cameron circled his hands around, in a full sweat.

"Oh great, Captain Spazz is here," Zoe groaned.

She took the camera out of Cam's hand and plugged it into the computer's USB drive. "How long of a video do we want?"

Knock. Knock

Mr. Docker entered the production studio.

"Is Chen still alive in here?" Mr. Docker asked.

"He needs a chill pill," Zoe laughed.

"Mr. Docker, we're fine. It's fine, I'm fine. We're all fine. Everything's fine."

"Oh boy," Mr. Docker said. "Listen, I know you guys are pulling for a certain outcome, but I just want to remind you that we need this special to be unbiased."

"Obviously," Cameron pulled at his hair.

"I'm just saying, I don't want this to turn into the underdog hour on Moose Patrowski. I'm not so sure that's what we're going to get out of this."

"You still don't think Moose is going to win?" Zoe asked. She never turned her head away from the computer screen. She already started sifting through the raw footage they collected from the classroom voting. She started chopping scenes and adding fade-ins and outs. "Do you think it will be Macie?"

Mr. Docker paused. He scratched his beard and opened his mouth, then closed it. He shifted his weight around and nodded to Cameron, "Just make sure we don't forget about Glenda." And with that he walked out of the studio and shut the door.

"Docker thinks Glenda is going to win?" Zoe asked Cameron.

"He just wants the broadcast to be unbiased. I don't blame him with this going on. Look at those two idiots out there," Cameron signaled for Zoe to look at Isaac and Alyssa in the broadcast room.

Isaac rested a hand on Moose's shoulder as he went through the script and coached Moose up on ways to answer. Alyssa and Macie were on the far end of the broadcast desk taking selfies together, reviewing the selfies, deleting them, and taking them again. Glenda sat in the middle of the table reviewing her acceptance speech.

"Hmm, he has a point," Zoe shrugged and went back to her computer monitors.

"How much footage we do have of Glenda's homeroom?" Cameron paced the room.

"None," Zoe answered.

"What? We don't have her homeroom footage?" Cameron slammed a hand on the table. He flipped the speaker switch so his voice could be heard in the broadcast studio, "Camera-one, uh Chris, right? Chris can you—Kyle sorry. Sorry, I need you in here please."

The sixth grade camera operator, Kyle, sprinted to Cameron's command. Cameron met him in the doorframe with a portable camera in hand. "I need you to go set this up on a live feed in Glenda's home room. Stat."

"Uh," Kyle fidgeted. "Like what do you mean?"

"My gosh, man!" Chen ripped his glasses off. "Have you ever watched a championship game broadcast? A March Madness selection committee? College bowl game announcement?"

"Yeah."

"Like that, I want it set up like that."

"I'm still not sure wh—"

"—At the front of the room, wide shot, set it high, so it's coming down. We want the bird's eye view of the live action. So, when we announce the winner we can see the whole classroom react. Hurry. Go. No more questions. Hurry and get back here."

Cameron turned with his hands spread arm's length on both sides scoffing to Zoe, "Is this amateur hour?"

"Yikes, Captain Spazz, the kid is in sixth grade, he doesn't know—" Zoe cut herself off. "Speaking of amateur hour, look at this footage we have off Budgies and Alyssa's field cam. What is this?"

Zoe referred to the incident when Alyssa got so frustrated with Isaac, she forgot to end the recording. What Zoe saw on her monitor B, was the shaking camera held at about elbow height. Then it dropped to knee height and banged around while Isaac and Alyssa exited the classroom. For a tech expert like Zoe, watching the footage made her skin crawl.

"Oh my gosh! Did she literally walk down the entire hallway recording?" Zoe put her hand over her mouth laughing. "We have to show this to Budgies."

"Not right now; quit screwing around! We have fourteen minutes before this broadcast starts. Get serious."

"Hey guy, I'm telling you right now you need to cool it. Go take a lap."

"I'm not taking a lap! Not now. There's no time, Zoe."

"I need to finish this montage reel and you're stressing the crap out of me," Zoe said. "I need five minutes. Go take a lap."

Cameron put his hands on his hips to think it over.

"I'm serious dude," Zoe said with her hands up. "You have way too much nervous energy right now. I need you to leave the room so I can finish this. Go find the ballots or something."

"That's right!" Cam snapped his fingers. "The ballots! Who has the ballots? Where are the ballots?" Cameron stormed out of the room and continued his questions down the hallway. "Mr. Docker? Where's Mr. Docker? We need the ballots."

"He just walked out the hall," Isaac pointed from the studio. Isaac looked into production room to gauge Zoe's level of reaction. She seemed unfazed, head buried between the computer monitors.

Cameron slammed both doors down the center and walked out of the library, for that is where the broadcast room was stationed, and into the main hall. He turned his head both ways, like in a high-speed chase, "Mr. Docker!" he rushed down the hallway.

"Mr. Docker! There you are," Cameron gasped in relief.

Mr. Docker shook hands with Ms. Lungar who handed him an envelope, and if Cameron hadn't had his hands on his knees while he wheezed for air, he may have noticed Ms. Lungar nod to Mr. Docker while she turned away.

She didn't acknowledge Cameron, but that wouldn't have been weird. The vice principal and the news director had a long history of friction ever since last year when Cameron usurped her authority. He went directly to Principal Wallney for a petition signature to approve students wearing their club sport jerseys to school on a Friday. Lungar already gave him a hard "No" as the jerseys were not school affiliated, and more importantly, a gross violation of the school's uniform policy. Wallney signed the petition not caring either way, and bought Cameron's pitch that it supported the well-roundedness of student athletes and community participation. Cameron didn't even have a team jersey to wear; he simply wanted to prove to Lungar that he could get things done. Cameron agreed to toss the petition request if Lungar agreed that advanced PLAN broadcast classes could be taken as a double period instead of a music elective. Their relationship was dicey ever since.

So no, Cameron didn't notice the wink, and didn't think it odd at all that Lungar scampered away quickly avoiding any interaction with him.

"I've been," Cameron gasped again, "Looking for you, we need—"

"—Yes Chen, I've got the results sealed and ready to go," Mr. Docker jiggled the envelope. "Now, I know you're buddy in there wants to be the one to read them, but I think this is for Alyssa."

"What? Why? Isaac's been all over this election, he deserv—"

"—We both know Mr. Budgies has done a lot more than *covered* this election. And to be quite honest, I'm surprised you decided to go along with the Patrowski campaign."

Cameron's heavy breathing stopped; he stood up to explain to Mr. Docker, but he wasn't sure exactly what to say.

"Oh don't worry, I'm not upset. You're not the first reporter who tried to make his own story," Mr. Docker handed the envelope to Cameron. "But I don't want you and Budgies giving the new president a hard time, you understand?"

Cameron checked his watch. He grabbed the envelope from Mr. Docker and slammed into the library doors. It's a *pull*. He pulled the door handle and he entered.

"Remember to breathe!" Mr. Docker called after him as the doors shut.

Chen waived the envelope over his hands while he entered the studio, and with his other hand he signaled for everyone to take their places. He gave the camera kid a thumbs-up as he returned from his expedition. One would think Cameron had all the curiosity in the world to find out whose name was written on the envelope, but the reality was, Cameron didn't give a rat's ass who won. In his opinion, which no one asked for, the junior high student body principle is about as impressive a title as winning a superlative for "best hair." *Coincidentally, whoever's name was written inside this envelope would likely claim that designation too*, he laughed at his own joke.

All Cameron cared about was that the production, the show, and that the delivery of the name-any name would wow the audience. His job was to capture the moment, regardless of what the moment entailed. Besides, Moose had to win. All the polls, and nearly every voter Cameron talked to outside of the 8th grade girls' demographic claimed Moose. It'd be a landslide.

CH 15

Chen stepped into the broadcast studio with results in hand. *What was the point of trying not to smile?* He bit the inside of his cheeks as hard as he could, but Cameron was no poker player; he had something to say and it showed. He walked in like he was sucking on a lemon sour.

The camera operator in the room, and the candidates saw his smug face and the envelope he held. It would have been logical for them to assume Cameron Chen entered with the hubris of an Oscar presenter because he was holding the results. But Cameron didn't care about the results. Only Isaac knew that look, and Zoe. This was Chen's bad news face. More particularly, it was the ear to ear, beaming beacon of light, suppressed smile, the neon sign of "here it comes" face, that he reserved almost exclusively to drop bombs on his best friend.

"Oh my gawsh!" Macie Neadle said. She shimmied her shoulders. "Are those the results?"

Oblivious to the conversation that just took place outside, the decision of who would read the results was already made, but Alyssa recited a mantra to herself.

I will announce the winner, she bit her lip and felt the tingling rush throughout her body while she gazed upon the envelope. *This is my story to tell. I will announce the winner.* Alyssa knew from years of watching award shows, that often the announcement of the winner of an award could be just as memorable as the winner itself. Alyssa did not take note the fact that the most memorable announcements of winners are because the announcer made some embarrassing error. Alyssa didn't have time or interest for such details.

Arm fully extended, Cameron lowered his hand from the shoulder socket to Isaac. For a half-second, Alyssa felt the drop of her heart hit her tailbone. But in one motion, Cameron rotated his arm, still at the shoulder joint, never breaking eye contact with Isaac, until he said, "Alyssa, you have the honors."

"Dramatic much?" Isaac asked Cameron.

"Whoa! Whoa! Whoa!" Cameron lurched forward to Alyssa and slapped the envelope down to the desk. "Not yet. You have to read it live." Cameron was well aware how memorable a botched envelope read can be, and he didn't want to throw out that possibility.

"Oh what?" Moose ached. "Come on, let's look."

"We have a full show to do here, people. Okay, let's go-go-go, let's go. We're live in 60 seconds!" Cameron clapped himself out of the studio and into the production room.

"Live in three ..."

The black lens, gateway to the eyes of the world, fixated its gaze on Isaac Budgies.

" ... two..."

A sniff, a swallow, and a smile.

"... one."

Fade in camera-one.

"Good afternoon Pine Lakes Academy. And welcome to our Special Announcement Broadcast. I'm Isaac Budgies."

Cut to camera-two.

"And I'm Alyssa Sonoma."

Back to One.

"And we are joined here with three very special guests, familiar to all of you by now, I'm sure."

Cut to camera-two: Isaac's voiceover, tight zoom on Macie. "Macie Neadle."

Cut to camera-one: Isaac's voiceover, tight zoom on Moose. "Moose Patrowski." He waives.

"Nice," Chen comments from the production booth.

Cameron and Zoe are alone in the booth when Mr. Docker enters silently. He turns the corners of his lips down and shakes his head once. "No problem," he says without words. "Just observing." Mr. Docker leans against the wall for a front seat of the show.

Cut to camera-two: Isaac's voiceover, tight zoom on Glenda. "And Glenda Howard." She pumps a double thumbs-up.

"I voted for her," Zoe whispers to Chen.

Cut to camera-three: Wide shot, full table.

"Thank you Isaac, and welcome everyone, to the show we've been anticipating for weeks," Alyssa smiled. Zoe puts a smile face emoji on the teleprompter to remind Alyssa to smile. Alyssa would not let Macie Neadle steal her thunder, not yet at least. *Sure, Macie might be the new class president, but I'm still going to be the one on the news everyday.*

"So guys, are you excited the wait is finally over?" Alyssa asked.

"Let's just get it over with," Moose said to the wrong camera. The camera operator pointed Moose to look at the correct camera. "Let's just get it over with."

"I'm having a lot of fun," Glenda admitted. "But I'm glad the campaigning is over."

"Well, if Macie has nothing to add, let's take a look back at the campaign memories." Isaac clicked his index card on the desk.

The screen faded to black. It queued ready to run the montage clip Zoe managed to whip together in less than 20 minutes. It was complete with an emotional instrumental background.

After a beat, once the video started to play, Isaac flipped his notecard over to show Alyssa it was blank. Unimpressed, she rolled her eyes.

Cut to montage footage:

On screen, viewers saw flashed memories of the candidates waiving to the camera. As if anyone needed a reminder from three days ago, some students laughed at Moose's funny tie-dyed outfit. Zoe and Cameron, and even Mr. Docker, were smart enough to know that while stuff like this aired, most students were whispering and giggling with their friends, paying zero attention. But the work isn't always about the students entirely. They have a duty to also entertain the teachers, and staff.

Plus, there was an understanding of the undeniable quality of the production. Zoe's work, like the current montage, was so well done, that it deserves time be wasted from class. And all students agreed they'd rather not be paying attention to a news announcement broadcast, than be not paying attention to their teacher. So in their own unique way, Zoe knew the students appreciated her work. That nearly no one knew the work was hers, mattered not.

Fade in to camera-three: tight shot of Isaac and Alyssa only.

"Wasn't that something, Isaac?"

"It just reminds me how lucky we are to be a part of such a great place as Pine Lakes Academy."

"Sure does."

"Well, Alyssa, candidates? I think we've waited long enough."

"Isaac are you saying you want to know what I've got in this envelope right here?"

Gosh! Why does she have to have a boyfriend? Isaac wondered. *The way she smiled right there, she's a natural.* Isaac knew Cameron wrote the question and Zoe inserted the smile emoji as a prompt, but he ignored these facts, focusing only on the result.

"I don't think I can wait much longer," Isaac said, turning to her, hoping perhaps his comment was transparent enough to show his underlying plea while sticking to the topic at hand. *I think she'll get the hint.*

She didn't. The comment went over Alyssa's head.

"Okay, Zoe," Cameron said from inside the booth. "We want to do a few quick solo shots of each contestant. Alyssa—hopefully—knows she needs to hold it here for just a few beats.

Cut to camera-one: Zoom in on Moose, his mouth is open, he's staring off into something in the distance, He does not have the face of an eager contestant. Moose looks as if he was in mid conversation and forgot what it was he was going to say next. He sits digging through the depths of his cluttered mind trying to find the thought. His is the face most people make when they're nervous.

Cut to camera-two: Zoom in on Glenda Howard, she smiles and gyrates her neck in anticipation, and crosses her fingers. She mouths, "So exciting," to the camera.

Cut to camera-one: Zoom in on Macie Neadle, her arms are crossed, and she's biting her lip. This is perhaps the same face the woman had while she waited for King Solomon to make his famous slice. This was not the look of a friendly face.

"Okay, let's cut to a quad screen, I want camera-three, wide on the whole table, in the top left, and then the live feeds of each contestant home room on the other corners. Now," Cameron commanded.

"Ten bucks she can't open it," Zoe whispered.

"And the winner; your newest Pine Lakes Academy Student body president is."

Of course she can't freaking open it! Isaac groaned internally. *I'm sure those two are cracking up in there. But she's so hot.*

"Knew it," Zoe said.

"Quiet, this is it."

"Sorry guys," Alyssa showed both rows of her teeth. Then tore the envelope open.

"Glenda?" Alyssa asked pushing the card away. Then she recoiled, realizing her error instantly. With adjusted excitement she said, "I mean, And. Your new, student body president is Glenda Howard!"

Alyssa's eyes scanned Macie Neadle up and down for vital signs. *Is she pissed? She's pissed. Oh my gosh, yes! Freaking yes.* Alyssa thought to herself. *Do I look upset for her? Am I being a good fake friend? Does she know I didn't vote for her? You can't have it all, Macie. Karma, I love you.* Alyssa motored these thoughts in a half-millisecond while she looked back to smile at the camera, a real pure satisfied smile.

In the upper right corner, the live cam showed Glenda's homeroom raise their hand in silent jubilee.

"No way," Zoe gasped mesmerized by the screen. "Camera-one, cut to Glenda!"

Glenda shook the excitement out of her fingers.

"What?" Moose groaned; his voice picked up off-camera.

"It's me?" Glenda stopped shaking her fingers. "It's really me? Wow," Glenda composed herself, adjusted her glasses, and smiled.

"Unbelievable," Moose is heard off-camera again. He's also making a lot of noise moving around in his chair.

"Thank you, thank you to all the Pine Lakes Academy students who voted. This is the best school and I'm going to help make it even better for all of you."

Isaac hadn't moved. He sat, with a half smile, but sucking in hard on his lips from the inside of his mouth and his head hung somewhat tilted to one side. He lost. But technically, he reminded himself, he won. Because if Macie Neadle wasn't class president, then Alyssa might not need the additional status boost of dating a high schooler. So he ultimately got the results he wanted: a better chance to date Alyssa. But Glenda winning also meant Moose lost, which means Isaac was wrong. Isaac needed to keep his eye on the prize, but he wasn't the type of person who lied to himself. *The truth is that I lost. I lost the election to Glenda?*

"You guys lost?" Zoe asked Cameron in the booth.

"Queue to Isaac," Cameron ignored her. He hoped Mr. Docker wasn't paying attention.

"Thank you again to all the candidates, and a special thanks to all of you out there who voted," Isaac turned to Glenda with an outstretched hand. "And congratulations to you, Ms. President."

"Thank you, Isaac. Thank you so much to everyone, I can't wait to serve you as president."

Isaac squared himself to the camera, "This concludes our special announcement presentation. Tomorrow, we'll tell you what we learned today." Isaac bit his lip and shook his head one time, just before the camera cut to black.

CH 16

Moose Patrowski fussed with his clip on mic, struggling to pull it off his shirt. He jumped from his chair, flailing his arms around while he tripped over the cords. "There's no way," he insisted.

"Alright dude, settle down," Isaac tried to calm the awkwardness filling the room.

Luckily, Moose's temper tantrum took some of Macie's focus off of her so-called friend, Alyssa. Elated, relieved, overjoyed, guilt-ridden, but mostly happy, Alyssa summoned all her strength to swell with tears for Macie. Macie, who could count on one hand the instances in her life where she did not get what she wanted, was in full on water-works meltdown. Macie's make-up smeared, and spit clung from her top lip connecting to her lower lip. Not getting what she wanted fried her circuits. She was losing her mind; it was loud, and unsightly.

Finally untangled, Moose looked to Isaac for answers.

"There's no way man!" Moose pointed to Isaac. "Are we still recording?"

"No, dude, but you need to chill."

"No offense Glenda, I mean, way to go, but dude, Isaac. There's no way. We had all the numbers."

This bozo, Isaac thought. *Why don't we turn the cameras back and make an announcement to the whole school that I helped you? Not that I wasn't allowed,* Isaac rationalized to himself. *But, I mean, now that he lost, I can't be associated with a losing candidate.*

Mr. Docker left the production booth and practically skipped into the filming studio to address the students. The volume lowered slightly as soon as Mr. Docker entered the room. His purpose was equal parts consoling Macie, getting Moose to control himself and calm down, but first, congratulating Glenda.

"This is great," Zoe laughed to Cameron looking upon the chaos in the filming room. Zoe caught eyes with camera operator Kyle, and she swirled her finger in a circle telling him to make sure he recorded everything going on in the room.

"I will cherish this footage," she laughed again.

Cameron pulled at his hair, slow, and long, and exaggerated, as if he had a thought deep in his brain and literally had to pull it to the surface of his mind. He paused. Then he sat down. Then stood up again.

"Oh my gosh," Zoe raised her palms, "Would you freaking spill it already?"

"He's not wrong," Cameron said through his fingers over his mouth.

"What do you mean?"

A long inhale through flailing nostrils, "I mean, this fumbling baboon in there has a point. I thought he was going to win. Didn't you?"

Zoe looked on to the green room while Moose packed up his things, unable to storm out like he wanted to because of the microphone cords, "Unfortunately, yeah. I kinda did."

Practically reading their minds, Isaac Budgies looked through the glass into the production room at his two best and only real friends. Isaac had his hands on his hips, but raised them with a shrug, "How?" he mouthed.

"Very well done, Ms. Howard," Mr. Docker said with three or four claps. "Congratulations."

"Oh thank you, Mr. Docker. You know, I said to myself, I just have to stay positive. Stick to my notes. Keep to the plan. That's what I said for the last few weeks. Because you never know what can happen with a positive attitude and organized notes."

"I agree, I'm very proud for you," Mr. Docker replied.

And catching himself before really letting the compliments flow, he made a somber face at the sight of Macie's running mascara. Noticing for the first time how much mascara Macie wore: way too much. Two thick lanes of black stripes ran down each cheek to her chin. *Kids these days,* he thought to himself. *Well, I've met her mother; I see where she gets it.*

"Okay Macie," Docker said with his hands back in his pockets. "This is nothing to be so upset about. Either of you two." He added towards Moose.

"I'm just, like, so embarrassed," Macie cried. "Everyone basically hates me."

"Macie, it's okay," Alyssa said struggling to wipe the grin off her face.

"Macie, nobody hates you," Docker white-lied.

"Like how can I even like show my face in this school anymore?"

"Alright, I'm going to go get someone for you," Docker walked backwards toward the door. *This is why I work with the nerdy ones.*

"I want a recount! We're doing a recount! How can I get a recount?" Moose demanded.

Docker stopped, "Not possible—I mean, what? Why?"

Sometimes, the human's sub-conscious picks up on a thing that the conscious person doesn't register. At least not at first. There is that awkward second, when the heart feels like it pounds a little harder for just one beat, but it goes ignored. This is what happened to Isaac when he didn't notice the way Mr. Docker shut down Moose's requested instantly.

"I think there's been a mistake. No offense, Glenda."

"None taken, Moose."

"But there's no way she could have beat me!"

"All votes are final, Moose," Mr. Docker said an octave lower than normal. "We've moved on."

"But what if there was a mistake? I want a recount."

"There was no mistake. Don't be a sore loser, congratulate Glenda and thank you're lucky stars you don't have to go to any morning meetings."

📷 📷 📷

After the final bell of the day, throngs of disappointed students offered their condolences to Moose.

"You got robbed, dude," some would say.

"Recount!"

"I voted for you Moose."

And stuff like that.

"What the hell, man?" Moose demanded to Isaac, red in the face. Causing what some would describe as "a scene."

"Calm down, big guy."

"Screw you, Budgies. I got robbed and you know it. Right, Chen?"

Cameron and Zoe approached for support. The early lingerings of a crowd started to form. Whispers scattered like echoes down the hall.

"I want a recount. This is total B.S., No way I lost to a chick."

"What is that supposed to mean?" Zoe stepped in.

"Okay everybody just calm down, come over here," Cameron motioned them down the hallway towards the music room to avoid the students, both those trying to watch the drama, and the vast majority clamoring for the exits.

"Look, just come in here," Isaac waived to the teacher's bathroom through the auditorium.

"We can't go in there," Moose recoiled.

Cameron did a quick look around for any teachers and swiped his student fob against the door lock and they rushed in.

"How the heck?"

"Keep it to yourself, Moose," Isaac explained.

"Should she be in here?"

"Look, we've decided to back you," Chen said.

"What do you mean?"

"Dude," Zoe smacked her forehead. "With the recount."

"Okay great, let's do it. Meeting over."

"It's not that simple," Isaac placed his hand on the door.

Moose took a step back, "What are you dorks talking about? Yeah. It is. You walk up to Mr. Docker and you say you're doing a recount. Make it a story."

"It would be a great story," Chen smiled. He motioned with his hands in the air, painting the headline, "Election Controversy: Moose Wants to Count Again." Cameron smiled, "Which is kind of ironic, you know?"

Zoe chuckled, "Yeah cause—" But she stopped herself.

"Cause what?"

"Doesn't matter. The point is, we're going to move forward with the recount story," Isaac explained. "But, first I gotta ask you something Moose: Are you sure you want us to look into this?"

"Hell yeah, man. Why wouldn't I? I'm not a loser." Moose puffed his chest.

"I'm saying, think about it. If there *was* a mistake, that would mean you would be the new school president."

Moose nodded.

"It's a lot of work," Zoe offered.

Moose scratched his head. "No way I lost to a girl. Count 'em again."

"Real sophisticated," Zoe shook her head.

CH 17

Zoe had to be the one to say it. If it came from Cameron, it would be too obvious that it was actually Isaac's idea. There was no way Isaac could introduce it because that would all but cement the truth behind the rumors that he pulled the strings for Moose to win. Zoe knew it had to be her. She made sure Cameron and Isaac knew for the record, she voted for Glenda. She was only going to suggest they go with the "Recount" headline because it was good for ratings. Plus, if it worked for keeping their parents' butts glued to the couch, it would work on the students too, right? Recount stories always keep people tuned in.

Zoe raised her hand at the next day's class session when they were going over the stories for the next news cycle. Zoe raised her hand out to the side the way a server carries a tray of dishes. People thought Zoe did this because she was lazy and edgy, but actually Zoe always liked the image that her ideas were like entrées for the mind. She was serving up something delicious, and maybe she knew it made her look kind of edgy too.

"Oh, Ms. Vernar?" Docker called on her. "Please take your gum out."

Zoe swallowed, "It's pretty obvious the next headline is to go with the recount thing, right?"

"And what exactly is this *recount* thing?" Mr. Docker asked putting his hands in his pockets.

"Moose freaked out after the results show, and he demanded a recount," Alyssa Sonoma jumped into action.

Alyssa also recognized this story as great way to stir drama. With Macie going down in flames, the last thing in her way of world domination was being recognized as the number one chair for the morning news. Eighth grade was starting out as the best year of her life.

Sure, I fumbled opening that stupid envelope, but like who wouldn't? The thing was like literally cemented shut. No one ever remembers who opens the envelopes for that kind of stuff anyways. Alyssa thought.

Alyssa planned on riding this hot streak to the very end. She would start high school as the most popular girl in school, and that meant ending eighth grade with the crown. Getting in front of a recount story sounded like a great way to further boost her fame.

"No. I don't think so," Mr. Docker waived it off.

Cameron wasn't in the green room yesterday, so he didn't get the chance to experience Mr. Docker saying no to an idea. Docker loved the gang. Docker said "No" to maybe three or four ideas tops that they came up with in the last two years. Back in sixth grade, Docker said no to doing a smear campaign against one of the schools chef's for having bad fingernails. Docker also nixed Chen's plan to run with a story that the athletic director deserved to be fired after Pine Lakes went two years in a row for the first it time in 50 years without a playoff win in any boys or girls sport. And there was of course, the time Docker promptly pulled the plug on a video-piece Isaac and Chen put together where they snuck into their cross-town rival junior high for a day and tried to paint the school in a bad light.

But usually, Mr. Docker was always there for them. He always said "yes." He said yes to their idea about running a sports segment. He green-lit the late night talk show premise when interviewing students from the school play. He encouraged them to follow up on whether there was a PTA agenda to limit the number of slow songs at the school dance. Mr. Docker always backed them, but not on this. And it felt different.

Jenny Towlel raised her hand to speak.

"What? Why not?" Cameron chimed in.

"They're over the election. It's gone stale," Mr. Docker said.

Jenny flayed her hand back and fourth.

"I disagree. People love the recount," Cameron insisted. "I'm too young to remember the Bush vs. Gore recount saga, but I know the big media ran advertisements off that story for months. The Trump vs. Hilary campaign pumped pharmaceutical commercial sales for like four full years after that election," Chen continued. "And then they double-downed on it again. People love watching a good election scandal."

"Parents maybe," Mr. Docker shook his head, "Not students."

Jenny finally resolved internally, she was going to do what everyone else did and just speak without being called on. She opened her mouth and—

"—I think there's something there," Isaac blurted while raising his hand, just before Jenny could say anything.

He couldn't sit on his hands any longer. It killed him not to speak. A debate? An argument about whether a story exists and whether there is any interest to run with it? He had to.

Jenny put her hand down frustrated.

"Of course you do. Your candidate lost," Alyssa rolled her eyes.

"He beat Macie," Isaac whipped back.

"Not if they counted wrong."

"Look, Mr. Docker, see? There it is. Right there," Chen pointed at Alyssa. "If 'they' counted wrong. The teachers! Kids want to know if the teachers made a mistake."

"I don't think anyone cares."

"How can you say that?" Chen gasped.

Jenny raised her hand again.

"I agree with Zoe and Cam on this, Mr. Docker," Alyssa said in a more level and calm tone. She knows moving one's face too much causes wrinkles, "And I almost never agree with them, but I think there's a story here."

"It's either a great idea for her, or a bad idea for me, but we agree," Chen said.

"Gee, thanks?" Alyssa said across the room, this got some laughs.

Alyssa noted her sarcastic humor had positive feedback from her peers. *Why does everything have to be funny?* She wondered. She once tried to research ways to incorporate comedy when interacting with her classmates to increase popularity, but she discovered she was only funny when she was being mean. *Jokes are stupid.*

"Listen, I don't like it. Glenda won. We're off the election. It's old news. Does anyone have anything else?"

Cameron, Zoe, and Budgies exchanged shrugs. Even allowing a stray glance to Alyssa. How did Docker not bite at an idea for a recount? Isaac sniffed; he smelled a story. Isaac also pretended not to think about the fact that pulling Alyssa into the group to help uncover an investigative news story was a surefire way to get some quality time with her. Maybe they'd even hang out on Friday night. What if she invited the gang over to her house, with her huge basement? And if it were just the four of them, Cameron and Zoe would probably start—

"Isaac?" Zoe asked.

Isaac shook his himself back to reality.

"Don't get too far ahead," Zoe winked.

She knew. But Cameron knew too, and Alyssa had a good hunch. There was something going on with the recount. Docker denying it only fueled their curiosity.

CH 18

After the bell, the PLAN class students packed up to hurry to their next period, but Cameron, Budgies, and Zoe stayed behind. Alyssa noticed, so she stayed too. Jenny also noticed, but she had gym class next and they were doing swimming. She'd need as much time as possible to get changed. Reluctantly, Jenny left the room. Mr. Docker pretended not to notice as he took careful time pinning up a few blank notecards to the corkboard. He addressed them before turning around.

"I didn't know we were having a meeting today," Mr. Docker said with a smile when he spun. He wiped his hands on the back of his blazer, and then raised his long arms wide.

"So, what's going on?"

"You tell us," Cameron started. "Why don't you want us doing this recount story?"

"Same reason I said in class; it's stale."

"We don't think so," Alyssa add.

We? She's using we *now?* Isaac noticed. *This is my chance. I cannot screw this up. We gotta do this story together. We're on the same team and I'll win her over. I'll be funny and interested in her. Thank you, Mr. Docker!*

"*We* think students want to know who the real winner was," Isaac said, stressing the *we* wanting Alyssa to see that it was him and her together; they were a *we*.

"It was Glenda," Docker lost his smile. "Listen, I am not having any more discussion on this, we're not creating a scandal out of thin air."

"But what if there as a mistake?"

"There was no mistake. Trust me, there was no mistake. That numbskull, Moose, should be thanking his lucky stars he just dodged all the responsibility he can possibly handle."

"*We* want to look into a recount," Isaac said.

"I am not running any kind of story about any recount, and that's final." Mr. Docker walked closer to their desks. He towered over them, with a slight bend to stress from how far his powerful orders came down. "Tomorrow, we're shifting gears from the election, and starting on whether there should be a uniform petition."

"But Glenda didn't have that as part of her platform," Zoe said.

"What do I always tell you guys? 'The news creates the news.' We start with the uniforms tomorrow and the debate will spark itself. It'll be the new thing."

He paused to let his wisdom sink in.

"Anything else?" Mr. Docker asked.

"I guess not," Isaac said getting up from his desk.

"Hey listen, guys," Mr., Docker said. His smile was back, but looked heavier for his cheeks to keep it still. "This is my last year with this team. We have a lot of great stories, and a lot of good news left to cover. I want this to be our best year yet. It's time to move on to our next narrative. That's all."

"We'll do the uniforms," Isaac said. "What's your take on them?"

"It doesn't matter what I think, it's a rule for the students," Docker nodded. "You guys cover it with any angle you want. Obviously, the school administration is never going to change the rule. Not to mention the PTA would be against it. But it's a good story for a cycle."

"Thanks Mr. Docker," Cameron fixed his glasses.

"Okay, get out of here," he waived them out of the room.

Zoe didn't speak up. She got out of her desk and walked to the door just like the others. But she looked only to Cameron, and in the special way that they always seemed to be able to, she spoke telepathically to him. And in Isaac's own special way, he could intercept such messages, and listen-in in their on conversation. While the four of them walked out the door, Zoe and Cameron decided they would in fact look into this recount situation. And Isaac decided it would be his idea.

Jenny Towlel popped out from behind the threshold in the hallway; she waited just around the corner. "I want in."

CH 19

The social make up of the junior high cafeteria, which is nothing more than a 21st century watering hole, is one of the most fragile ecosystems on earth. The illusion is that the lions, the popular and often meanest of the jungle, sitting together are the safest from ridicule and negative attention. Yet, as any student ever to sit down at a table alone will tell you, the safety is in the numbers alone. At a full table, regardless of who is there, a student is protected and can go unnoticed from insults, threats, or laughs. Wildebeests don't like all wildebeests, but one more wildebeest at the table is better odds for everyone that they're not the one to get eaten, or ridiculed.

It is the open chair that shines like a beacon for ridicule, endangering anyone near it. Isaac, Cameron, and Zoe each experienced an empty chair next to them, across from them, or surrounding them plenty of times. Luckily, in the last couple years of finding their place in the herd, with the nerds and the tech crew, plus the help of Isaac's face being the most recognizable in the school, they no longer feared the open seat at their table. They couldn't find anyone to fill it, but it didn't bother them as much.

The three sat in a corner in the raised eighth grade section of the cafeteria, separate from the underclassmen. They sat with a couple of the camera guys, but each table could seat eight. Isaac, Cameron, and Zoe's table never sat more than six or seven. The tech and camera guys would sometimes pile in together to play a game of cards, or debate super heroes. In those instances, Cameron, Zoe, and Isaac risked sitting at a table of only three. Sometimes Zoe would have a few of her girlfriends sit with them, but they often couldn't keep up with the pace of conversations.

The balance in the ecosystem of the watering hole rested on the fact that lions ate with lions, the zebras ate with zebras, and so on. Which is why when the popular lioness, Alyssa Sonoma, strutted over to one of the empty chairs at Isaac's table, everyone watched, and the humming buzz of voices went noticeably quieter.

Alyssa had a choice to make with all the eyes of her world watching: does she sit next to Isaac or Cameron? As if it was a choice, she took the chair open next to Cameron. The last thing Alyssa needed when trying to break a big story is that self-absorbed lunatic thinking they were going to be a team. Alyssa was no-sidekick. She really lucked out in all of this, too didn't she? Alyssa's thoughts went a million miles an hour. She knew enough about the polls and the votes, and the results, that Macie came in third. It was irrefutable. But she could "look into this recount" playing the cards like she's doing it for Macie. If anyone got screwed, it was Moose, but Macie thought it was her. Now, here comes Alyssa, the shining star and world's greatest friend, going to try and get a recount to happen. Little does Macie know, the recount is going to show that she came in *third*, which is even worse, and if those results are public, it would take months for Macie's social profile to recover.

"Something we can help you with Alyssa?" Cameron asked, instinctively scooting closer to Zoe when Alyssa sat down."

Isaac noticed the chair on his right was still empty. He and Alyssa made a flash of eye contact. It was long enough to tell Alyssa that Isaac got the message she sent by choosing the chair next to Cameron.

Alyssa waited for the murmuring in the lunchroom to pick-up, and once the volume spiked to its natural level, she leaned into the table.

"So, I did something like kinda a little cray, but I think I found something," she looked around the table. Then continued. "Obviously like, Mr. Docker doesn't want us doing the recount story, right? But I'm like 'Um why not Mr. Docker? Like what is the big deal, are you like hiding something?' You know? So I was like thinking like how are we like actually going to like get access to the votes, right?"

Cameron leaned his head forward, his glasses started to slide down his nose and he pushed them back with one finger to his forehead. *Nine likes*, he noticed.

"So, like after we left talking to Mr. Docker, I went into the admin office, and like I mean I'm in there all the time for news stuff or getting sick day passes, or whatever, right? So it's not really like they ask me what I'm doing in there. So like I go see if Ms. Lungar is in, but they go, 'Oh she's in the bathroom she'll be back in like ten minutes.' So, I like literally went into her office and—"

"—You snuck in her office!" Zoe gasped in a whisper. *Geez, this girl is crazy, but also good for her, I don't think I'd have the guts. Ew, stop. Why am I complimenting Alyssa Sonoma? She's the worst.*

"Yeah, like I figure like, if I'm going to be a sideline reporter, sometimes I'm going to have to do some investigative journalism, right?"

"Probably not," Cameron shrugged.

"So what happened?" Isaac asked.

"Well, so like I walk in there, and like no one is there, so I just like literally started looking through her desk, and literally this was sitting on the top of her desk." Alyssa reached for her backpack and started to unzip it.

"Oh-em-gee! You stole something from the vice principal's office?" Zoe spoke with her hand covering her mouth.

"Oh my gosh; no?" Alyssa rolled her eyes, and pulled out her phone. "But look at this like document, she had literally on her desk, guys."

"I can't believe you did that," Isaac smiled. "That is like James Bond stuff. Were you nervous?"

"I know, right? My armpits were like so sweaty."

Alyssa's eyes went super wide, she was just honest. Like actually totally honest... with Isaac Budgies! *No, no. I did not just let my guard down in front of Isaac Budgies. Never again.*

"But I figure, like if we don't take the risk, we're not going to get the story, right?" Alyssa rebounded.

"Unbelievable," Cameron handed the phone back Alyssa.

"Give it to me, I want to see it." Isaac reached out for Alyssa's phone. He was very tempted to look through it to see how his name was stored in her contacts.

"Alyssa, do you know what that is?" Cameron put both hands on his head.

Alyssa, looked intrigued, Cameron's body language and tone were negative and dismissive, but the adrenaline still flowed through her body from the rush of discovering some major big-time news.

"It looked like some sort of like secret rules book, doesn't it?"

"No. It's the Pine Lakes Student Constitution," Cameron put his elbows on the table. "It's posted on the school's website. It's a public document."

THWACK!

Alyssa practically gave herself whiplash from the extreme shift in her emotions from pride to embarrassment. Her cheeks went so red they could probably boil an egg. Even Zoe felt a little tiny bit sorry for Alyssa. Cam could have said that a little nicer. She went and took a major risk, not only to sneak into the vice principal's office, but also to come over to the table and show them. The least Cam could have done was let her off easy.

Oh my god, I am literally going to die of embarrassment at the loser table, Alyssa pained.

"Well hold on a second," Isaac, who would do anything to get this girl to like him, chimed in.

"I think there's something here. Look at this," Isaac zoomed in and passed the phone back over the table for the others to look at. "Lungar has a pen mark circled on the election rules. It says a president is selected by a reviewable majority vote of the students. She circled the word "reviewable." Cam, she was looking into the recount."

Alyssa hated what was going on inside her right now towards Isaac. He rescued her from embarrassment.

"Oh wow," Cameron confirmed. "I take it back. I think you found something."

Validation.

"Why would she have circled this?" Zoe asked.

Alyssa, didn't pay attention, she focused on her breathing to keep her cheeks from reddening. *You found something, you trusted your gut and found something. Calm down. Good job.*

"That's the question," Cam adjusted his glasses trying to read the full paragraph of the rule. "That's what we need to find out."

CH 20

"Oh no, I'm not doing that," Moose said.

Isaac and Cameron cornered him in the hallway just outside of the cafeteria.

"You have to. They won't do a recount unless you ask."

"Then you ask him, Chen." Moose shrugged.

"I wasn't a candidate, I have no standing to bring the complaint," Cameron replied. He spoke with a finger pointed at Moose the way a mother scorns a child. Nobody ever talked to Moose that way, especially his own mother.

"I've never met the guy," Moose said. "What do I do? I just walk into the principal's office and I say I want a recount?"

"Yeah," Isaac said. "But you need to do it like right now."

"We think Vice Principal Lungar is expecting you to ask for a recount," Chen explained.

"That some real investigating journalism there, Chen. Do you think it might be because me and everyone else in the school's been talking about it?"

"I'm not sure why, but if she has access to the votes, we need to get them recounted ASAP."

"Macie wants it more than I do. Why don't you just have her ask for a recount?"

"If Macie has half a brain, she'll know she came in last place. She's not going to ask. If there's no recount, that means you lost to a girl," Cameron said. Cringing to himself internally.

"Fine!"

📷 📷 📷

Moose walked into the door to Principal Wallney's office a half stride-length at a time. *What am I doing?* He wondered. *Recount? Do I even care? Did I even want to win? Did I want to lose? Most powerful kid in school, hell yeah I want to win.*

"I'm here to see Principal Wallney," Moose said to the first person he saw sitting behind the counter.

"I'll tell him you're here."

Moose noticed she didn't ask him for his name. *See? You think every kid who walks in here the lady behind the desk knows who they are? No chance. I'm Moose Patrowski; no chance I lost that election.*

Moose walked his way into Principal Wallney's office and could hear the sound of a baseball announcer coming from Wallney's phone. Moose didn't sit down, and Wallney didn't look up from his phone propped up on the front of his desk.

"Yeah?" Wallney asked. "Who said what this time?"

"What?" Moose took one more step into the office.

"Only time someone comes in here is cause someone said something or did something offensive, so what is it?"

"I just wanted to ask—"

Just then Macie Neadle barged through the door. She body-checked Moose in the doorway and pounded both of her hands down on Wallney's desk. Her make-up was halfway run down her face, dripping in tears, and probably some water applied in the girl's bathroom.

The receptionist followed shortly behind, "I'm so sorry sir, I couldn't stop—"

"We're recounting those votes! We have to! We have to!" Macie wailed on the desk.

Mr. Wallney pressed the button on his desk to call the receptionist in, realizing the receptionist was already in the room trying to pry Macie off his desk.

"What is going on?" Mr. Wallney asked, appalled at Macie's display, but also still somewhat interested in the baseball game.

"I'm not leaving until you promise me there will be a recount!"

Moose walked backwards out the door, slow and deliberately so as not to get roped into Macie's craziness. She seemed like she'd do a better job at getting this done than he would. But first he took a quick picture of Macie losing her mind.

"That's really not my depar—"

"Aaarrrghhhhhhh!" Macie screeched at the top of her lungs. It was such a high pitch, that others from the office came to the doorway expecting to witness a fire or perhaps a monster in the hallway.

"Stop it, stop it, holy sh—okay!"

Macie stopped yelling. She wiped her nose and said, "There's no way I lost that election. Will you order a recount?"

"Yes, just get out of my office right now! Everyone!"

The receptionist ushered Macie out by the shoulders.

"And shut my door!"

"I'm so sorry, sir," the receptionist said, closing the door.

"Thank you, Mr. Wallney," Macie said.

"Seven hundred and one more days. Seven hundred and one more days," Mr. Wallney said putting his feet on top of his desk.

🎥 🎥 🎥

Isaac sat up on the black granite sink inside his and Cameron's pseudo-private bathroom. Cameron leaned up against the opposite wall. They both just finished getting their report from Moose in between periods with only one class left in the day—English for Isaac and History for Cameron. The buzzing idea that Assistant Principal Lungar had the rules circled on her desk meant *something*, but they weren't sure what. Whatever it was, it was too important to wait to discuss after school, and much more important than anything anyone had to say in English or History. Especially History, that was old news. Cameron was in the business of new news.

"I just don't see what the story is," Isaac said. "She had them on her desk, so she was looking at them. That's not a headline."

"And definitely not something Docker is going to change his mind over."

"I mean, it's obvious she doesn't want Moose to have won," Isaac continued. "I guess probably no teachers wanted that."

"Not a story though, not a surprise." Cameron leaned forward and allowed himself to gently bang his back against the wall. "The real question is if you think she rigged the vote?"

"I was gonna say maybe she just straight up lied about who won. That's why she'd be nervous about having a recount."

"Actually that does make more sense," Chen admitted. *Wait, this was my idea, he's doing it again!*

"Well, if Moose comes through and demands the recount, the rules say the school has to give it to him. Docker's obviously going to want that on the news. We just can't let him know we're the ones who told Moose to ask."

FLUSSHHH!

Isaac and Cameron both jumped at the sound of the flushing stall behind the tile partition in the bathroom. They both bulged their eyes. Did the other one forget to check the bathroom was empty?

Cam bit his lower lip, opened his mouth wide and chomped his teeth closed quickly; Isaac could read his lips. Chen dropped his hands to his knees and peered under the last door, someone was in there. He made the same word again with his mouth.

The stall door swung open.

Mr. Docker walked out.

Isaac's stress hit him like someone dumped a bucket of hot water over him. He could only imagine where Cameron's spazz level was at. Isaac replayed the entire conversation in his head over and over again, *Did*

I say anything bad about Mr. Docker? Did I say anything bad about Mr. Docker?

Mr. Docker spoke while he finished tucking in his shirt to his trousers.

"I thought we talked about this already?"

Cameron didn't like that Docker entirely skipped why they were in the teacher's bathroom, how did they have access to the teacher's bathroom, what were they doing in the teacher's bathroom? None of that—he just went straight to the point. Not a good sign at all.

"And you agreed to drop it?" Docker continued.

Mr. Docker looked Cameron straight in the eye. Mr. Docker never looked so pissed before, almost rattled, the veins around his eyeballs popped; they had a yellow tint to them. Docker's cheeks were red too, and he stiffened his lips, then scratched his head. Chen continued to stand silent in the corner, but the blood seemed to be circulating once again because he finally moved, shifting his weight on his feet.

"You two think you know everything, don't you?"

He paused.

"I've been teaching for thirty years, don't you know I'm five steps ahead of you at all times?"

"Look we just thought," Isaac started.

"I know what you thought. And I know what you think you know. But you two don't know anything. Lucky for you, Macie Neadle just bailed you out. She put on quite the performance in Mr. Wallney's office and he's already told me we're doing a recount. So now we have to do it. But because you two deliberately disobeyed me, I'm giving it to Jenny."

"What? That's not fair!" Isaac shouted.

"It's done, Budgies. And if it weren't for Macie losing her mind about an hour ago, this would be a very different conversation. You're lucky she's the one who asked before Moose could get the words out of his mouth. But my hands are tied now. We're running the recount. With Jenny."

"Macie, huh?" Cameron scratched his head. "Why does she think? Well, duh."

"This whole thing is wasting everyone's time," Mr. Docker placed one hand on each of their shoulders. "Glenda was the right choice. We all know it."

He turned to the sink to wash his hands, after they'd been on their shoulders. "Listen to me next time, guys. I still know a few things you don't yet. Now get to whatever class you're supposed to be in."

CH 21

"And more on today's lead story, we go to Alyssa," Isaac said to the reflective glass lens.

"Count 'em again!" Sonoma smiled to the camera.

The camera operators could feel the tension in the room. Moose and Glenda Howard both sat at the table next to Alyssa but currently outside of the frame. Macie Neadle sat next to Isaac on the opposite end of the table. Mr. Docker said he didn't want to turn his show into a *Springer Episode*—whatever that meant—but if they wanted drama and anticipated an argument, he suggested a wide framed shot going across the room between Macie and Moose would make the most tense effect, and seem chaotic to viewers.

Glenda, smiling as usual, couldn't help but admire how Isaac carried himself. The guy didn't even have a scripted teleprompter. The teleprompter merely flashed a few bullet point items and Isaac could rift right there live on the air. Whereas, whenever anyone else spoke, they read off the carefully drafted script from the monitor, just below the camera.

I bet that's how Isaac has that more personal touch, Glenda said to herself. *Everyone else's eyes are always just a smidge off from directly looking at the camera. But Isaac Budgies stares right you. Huh, and I thought he was just looking at me.* Glenda laughed to herself. *I'm so bad.*

"Insert image top right of Alyssa," Cameron directed Zoe.

Zoe received a picture of Moose, submitted from a student, of him pointing furiously at Cameron Chen, red in the face, from their argument in the hallway after the election results. Zoe cropped it to remove the background and inserted Moose's demanding image over a stock photo of Pine Lakes Academy.

"We've all heard the outcry, seemingly the popular favorites, Moose Patrowski and Macie Neadle demanded a recount after being upset by Glenda Howard on Monday in the school's presidential election."

"Cut to camera-two on the turn," Cameron anticipated.

Alyssa turned to her left, as Zoe cut to the other view. "We're here this morning with president elect Glenda Howard, and her would-be usurpers, either Macie, or Moose."

"Cut to wide frame, camera-three," Cameron said.

"Obviously," Zoe whispered back.

"So Moose? After the election, reports swarmed in that you were seen in an altercation with Pine Lakes Academy News team members Isaac Budgies and Cameron Chen Monday after the election."

"Yeah, like pretty much everyone already knows that," Moose said.

"But Moose, why were you so upset?"

"Duh, cause I lost. I don't lose, especially to a gir—a nerd, no offense."

"None taken," Glenda smiled and shrugged.

"Moose, is it safe to say that you didn't expect to lose?" Alyssa asked.

"Obviously, no one expected me to lose—"

"—I did," Macie interrupted.

"Which brings me to Macie Neadle," Alyssa transitioned.

"Let's cut quick to close up on Macie; then back out to camera-one for a shot of just her and Isaac when his question starts," Cameron said into the headset.

"Good morning, Alyssa." Macie forced a smile.

For someone who forced smiles more often than she smiled for real, Macie should be better at them. Her hollow gesture went noticed by most students and nearly every teacher and staff. *This girl watches too much reality TV*, some of the adults thought, the ones that didn't watch too much reality TV themselves.

"Macie, so much of the immediate aftermath of the election seems to be focused on Moose Patrowski," Isaac said. "But you've not so quietly suggested a recount as well, isn't that right?"

"That's right, Isaac," Macie spoke without dropping her smile.

"My gosh, she looks like a ventriloquist dummy," Zoe whispered to Cam inside the production booth.

"But Macie, you think the recount is necessary because, in fact, you were the students' most popular vote?"

"Well yeah. Like, after basically hearing everyone like really upset about the vote, and like, I talked to literally so many people before the vote, they all basically said I was going to win. So it's kind of like a shock that I didn't."

"Cut to full panel," Cameron directed.

"So Glenda," Isaac said.

"Hi Isaac," Glenda was pretty sure she said, but who knows. *Oh my gosh, why is he making me nervous?*

"Good morning Glenda," he responded. "So Glenda, we have two students here who are both asking for a recount, as the person who won, how do you feel about that?"

"Isaac, and to everyone out there at Pine Lakes Academy, I told you in my campaign, that I will not only hear the voice of the students, but to actually listen. And I said I would do whatever I can in my power to help make Pine Lakes a better school for all."

"This is why I voted for her," Zoe said to Cameron.

"So you're okay with doing a recount?" Isaac asked.

"I wouldn't say I'm happy about it," Glenda smiled. "But if this is what the students want, what better than my first act as the president to comply? I just want the votes to be right, so that even if the people who maybe didn't vote for me see that I am keeping my word, maybe they'll be happy I won."

"Well Glenda, I'm sold," Isaac smiled into the lens.

"Me too," Glenda laughed. *Did that even make sense? Oh my gosh, chillax, Gee.*

🎥 🎥 🎥

The next day on the morning announcements, the news team kept the snowball rolling:

"Well this excitement is at an all-time level, now Isaac." Alyssa said. "We have some breaking news, we are going to go live to PLAN's very own Jennifer Towel who is standing by with Vice Principal Lungar and the technology department's Mr. Stentson. Jennifer can you hear us?"

"Split screen to live feed. Mute the side mics in green room, I want only Alyssa and Isaac live," Cameron directed.

Students sitting at their desks watched as the broadcast cut from a full shot of Alyssa Sonoma to a split screen of Alyssa, and the redheaded Jennifer Towel holding a mic standing in front of a large Xerox machine.

"Good morning Alyssa. That's right, I'm here live in the technology department with Vice Principal Lungar and Mr. Stentson," Jenny smiled.

"I can't believe we need to put Mr. Stentson on camera," Zoe cringed.

Mr. Stentson had a great face for radio. He wore smoggy coke-bottle glasses, and had the posture of someone who spent the last 30 years hunched over a computer. He had almost no hair left down the center of his head, but combed over long, thin, and greasy strands from both sides, in alternating rows, to cover this fact. Anyone who ever took Mr. Stentson's computer classes knew that his breath smiled like that tiny piece of steak you find a few days after dinner when you finally remember to floss. Students couldn't see Mr. Stentson's socks underneath his baggy pleated khakis, but he wore wool sucks that hung loose and saggy around his ankles.

Alyssa did not envy Jenny for having to stand next to him. But she was very jealous Jenny would be the one holding the mic for this very momentous announcement. There will definitely be a picture of this in the yearbook.

"Cut to full screen of Jenny's feed."

The students in their morning homerooms watched as the screen cut to a full shot of Jennifer Towlel pointing the microphone to Mr. Stentson. The recount story was a big deal, mostly because kids often heard adults talking about vote recounts, so it sounded important. The reality was, the longer the news announcements lasted, the less time they had for class. So they were very interested.

Look at this, Jenny thought to herself. *What a resume boost. I get to be here with a live shot of the recount results. At this time next year, nobody's going to remember who won the election, but they'll remember this scene in the yearbook. What everyone's going to remember is this shot right here, this interview. Me, Jennifer Towlel, looking so cute in my uniform and school blazer, narrating as these votes get fed through the machine. I mean, I don't know how the heck a scantron machine even works, but like if I don't know, I bet no one else does either. This is what they'll remember. This is how you become the host of Pine Lakes Academy News.*

Coming out of her own thoughts, Jennifer realized she had more to say and wanted to bring the mic back in to her mouth.

"What we are going to do is re-scan all the student votes into the scantron counter for live results,"

Jenny said. "Mr. Stentson, exactly how does the machine work?"

Mr. Stentson tapped on the microphone a few times before speaking, "Yes hello," he waived to the camera. "It's a machine," Mr. Stentson said putting his hands up to the air.

Jenny looked at Mr. Stentson, then to the camera operator, who rolled her finger through the air telling Jenny she'll need to dig a little deeper. This was not how they rehearsed the interview a few moments ago.

"I can see it's a machine, Mr. Stentson, but how does it work?" Jenny asked.

"We scan the votes in, just like you would load a photocopier, and you tell it to count the votes. Not too complicated."

Jenny's face started to match her hair color. *Do not humiliate me you old grouch!* She almost growled at him.

"Mr. Stentson, after the machine reads the scantrons, where do the results go?"

"I keep them in a file cabinet."

"No, not the physical results, I'm asking how will we know who wins?" Jenny smiled to the camera. "Remember, like we rehearsed?"

"Look over here," Mr. Stentson waived towards an ancient desktop computer. "I have a computer program set to read the votes, answer A is for whoever, B for whoever, and C for whoever—the machine reads each scantron and feeds the results into a computer program, which will automatically print the winner."

Jenny cringed when she pulled the microphone back to respond: it smelled exactly like Stentson's breath.

"Fascinating," she coughed.

Several students watching who knew the misfortune Mr. Stentson's lectures laughed at Jenny's facial expressions. Even some of the faculty held back laughs. Teachers have noses too. They once banned the guy from microwaving fish sandwiches in the teacher's lounge. He switched to hardboiled eggs.

Jenny collected herself and continued. This time shoulders square to the camera. "Alight, Mr. Stentson, it's time to recount the votes."

Until now, Ms. Lungar just stood motionless, smiling directly into the camera like a robot that got shut off mid-movement. She snapped out of her trance and raised a hand to Mr. Stentson.

"Thank you for helping us Mr. Stentson. And can you confirm you are running the votes through the machine exactly the same way you did last time?"

"Oh that's right," Mr. Stentson said. He walked over to his desktop computer. "I'll just finish inputting the machine's settings for the file, and here we go."

Mr. Stentson went his entire life finding a way to make those around him feel awkward in every moment. This interview was no exception. Still walking back to Jenny and Vice Principal Lungar, he grabbed towards the microphone in Jenny's hand and started talking. Startled, Jenny took a step back and lost her footing momentarily on the counting machine.

"Get ready to cut on my signal," Cameron said over the crew's radio.

"Do you think it will be different?" Zoe asked him.

Cameron looked out the window at Mr. Docker in the library. He had the feed on the library's TV but he wasn't watching. He looked content re-shelving some books.

"No," Cameron answered.

"Yes, Ms. Lungar, I can assure you this is the same way the votes were monitored the first time around. All 506 of them." Mr. Stentson gave a thumbs-up to either Ms. Lungar or the camera, but no one could be sure. "And here we go," he said, pushing a final button.

"Okay cutting back to camera-one for a full panel shot," Cameron directed. "And Jenny throw it to Isaac."

On camera, Jenny pressed one hand to her earpiece, very much aware of how official she looked. Viewers could hardly tell she practiced this exact move in the mirror nightly. "How are thing's looking back in the studio Isaac?"

"Thanks Jen, you can cut the tension with a knife in here. President elect Glenda, how you feeling?" Isaac asked.

"Pretty sweaty, actually," Glenda giggled.

I hate that I don't hate her, Macie thought.

"Anyone else? Moose?" Isaac asked.

"The people's champ ain't worried," Moose said.

"And you Macie?" Alyssa asked.

"I'm just like trying to figure out like what even is Moose doing here?"

"Says the girl in last place," Moose replied.

"Okay guys. Well Jen, it's getting chippy. Back to you," Isaac said.

"Once we go back to Jenny, I need cameras one, two, and three, to get a close-up on each of the candidates from right to left," Cameron said. "And cut to Jenny now."

"Thanks, Isaac. Time for the moment of truth. What we've all been waiting for. Mr. Stentson, please recount the votes!"

Jenny motioned for the camera to zoom in the on scantron sheets as they hummed through the machine. The machine vacuumed up the entire stack within seconds.

"Well, that was quicker than I thought," Jenny said into the camera.

"Story of my life," Mr. Stentson mumbled. "I'll just go over to the computer now and review the results."

Vice Principal Lungar waddled after him to the computer screen, "What does it say?"

"Quick cut to the 4-square panel," Cameron said inside the booth. "Keep live feed in fourth square."

Mr. Stentson leaned over to the computer screen and pressed a few buttons on the keyboard. Ms. Lungar shouldered him out of the way to see. She instantly regretted the movement, remembering she was on camera. She didn't know how to work the computer program, and didn't want to be seen on camera not knowing something. She pretended to click around on a few buttons, while the camera operator worked to get a shot of the computer screen. Jenny and Mr. Stentson stood behind Ms. Lungar's slumped body.

On the four square panel broadcasting into the classrooms: Macie Neadle preparing for the worst, started to muscle up tears; Glenda chewed on her thumb; Moose tried to make up his mind whether he actually wanted to win; and in the lower left, a tight shot of Jenny, Mr. Stentson and Ms. Lungar all leaning closer into the computer monitor. It only took 30 seconds for the voting ballots to run through the machine and Mr. Stentson to announce the results, but for those interested, it felt like an eternity.

Zoe, who is not superstitious at all, crossed her fingers wishing for Glenda. Cameron grabbed for a pencil and the nearest peace of scrap paper he could find to scribble some notes. He was more focused on whatever he was writing than the announcement. Zoe tried to read his chicken-scratch handwriting.

"Well, Mr. Stentson?" Jenny asked.

"Cameron, are we switching shots here?" Zoe asked out of the side of her mouth.

Cam was still writing. All she could see was scribbled numbers.

"What?" he said. "Oh shoot, okay, full shot to live feed now. Camera-two, get ready to pan back to Isaac and Glenda. It's going to be Glenda."

Zoe raised an eyebrow, puzzled at Cameron's confidence.

The camera operator zoomed in on Mr. Stentson, then zoomed out just a tad, and waited. Jenny put the microphone in front of Mr. Stentson, stretching her arm as much as she could.

"It's Glenda Howard, she won," Mr. Stentson said turning to the camera. He raised one thumbs-up slow and mechanically to about chin level. "63% voted for Glenda, 21% Moose, and 16% Macie. Glenda's the school president."

Off camera, there was an clearly audible "Perfect." It couldn't have been from Jenny, so that would mean Ms. Lungar said it, but there was no video evidence.

Inside Macie Neadle's own mental control room, a Cruella-DeVil type character opened the glass barrier to a red button, labeled *Meltdown* and proceeded to press the button. On screen, Macie Neadle lost her mind.

"16%? How is that freaking possible!?" she screamed through rushing tears and make-up. Too much for the seventh grade camera operator to handle, the screen started to shake on her corner of the square, because the kid holding the camera started laughing. This too was audible.

"Cut to Isaac and Glenda," Cameron said. "Shut him up!"

"Well," Isaac said. "It appears the votes were correct."

What he wanted to say was *Surprisingly*, but that would be rude to Glenda, and she looked so relieved.

"It's official," he continued. "Glenda Howard, congratulations on being the new president of Pine Lakes Academy."

Oh my gosh, Glenda thought. *Shake his hand. You can do this, just put your hand out there and shake his hand.*

Glenda reached out and started shaking her hand before Isaac actually made contact with her, but he was able to catch her hand and they shook. The entire moment would live on for all eternity in the archives of PLAN footage.

"Gee, thank you Isaac," Glenda said.

Then getting a grip on her faculties, she turned to the camera and straightened her spine. She said, "To all students of Pine Lakes Academy, I look forward to serving you as your next class president. Let's get this year started!" Then she gave a singular strong thumbs up, with her arm at a perfect right angle.

"Alyssa closes us out," Cameron directed.

"Thank you to all students and staff for tuning in to this special edition of Pine Lakes Academy News. Until next time, I'm Alyssa Sonoma..."

"Cut to wide shot of Isaac and Alyssa."

"And I'm Isaac Budgies. That's the morning news. Tomorrow, we'll tell you what we learned today."

"Cameron, how did you know?" Zoe asked.

Cameron took his headset off, without answering, and ran out the door to the studio to congratulate Glenda. Zoe knew something was wrong. Cameron never ran in his school uniform.

"Nervous energy," she said to no one. "Something's up."

CH 22

"He's been acting weird all day," Zoe explained. "This is especially weird for a Thursday night for him."

Zoe, Cameron, and Isaac sat in Cameron's basement. Mr. and Mrs. Chen collected a lot of movie memorabilia. Framed movie posters and cased wardrobe props lined the walls. The Chens were the "responsible" parents. They were always home. Yet, in all the times Isaac hung out in this lair, Mrs. Chen never once crossed the threshold of the steps. They had lots of privacy in the basement. Isaac eyed down his next shot on the pool table, while Cameron and Zoe sat next to each other on the couch.

Isaac wouldn't admit it, but it got old being the third wheel. He didn't like having to watch those two conoodling on the couch all the time. He usually stayed back and played pool, behind the couches, where he could still see the TV.

Sure, every once and awhile he'd try to be cool and bring a girl over, but she could never keep up with the banter of the other two. Which didn't always matter, because that wasn't the point of bringing a girl over to watch a movie in the Chen's basement. But still, Zoe with her sharp wit and sarcasm, Isaac desperately wanted to find someone like that. But where did they hide? Zoe was no help either. Sure, she had friends; some of them were fun, but unfortunately lacking in the visual effects department. If only he could get Alyssa to come to the Chen's house.

This third wheel session felt particularly uncomfortable. Isaac knew Cameron well, and he certainly knew well enough when this neurotic friend of his was troubled. After the broadcast on their bike ride home from school, Isaac watched as Cam rode home the entire time with his arms crossed and one hand over his mouth, deep in thought. He hardly touched the handle bars to make a turn. And now, he sat on the couch with his girlfriend and said next to nothing, and they were not locking lips.

Isaac also knew that getting Chen to spill the beans would be difficult. The kid was like quicksand: the harder you tried to squirm the issue out from him, the further down he buried it. Zoe knew this too, so they tried to wait it out, but two impulsive go-getters can only be patient for so long.

"Hey Cam?" Isaac asked.

Isaac kept his eyes on the pool table, trying to line up a shot. He nicked the queue ball and hardly scratched his target, sending the queue ball directly sideways into the corner pocket. Pool was not Isaac's best parlor sport.

"Cam?"

"What's up?"

"Are you thinking about when we need to start our social studies paper?"

"Cut it out, Isaac. I know what you're doing," Cameron said. "I told you guys I'm fine."

"Yeah he's fine," Zoe said. "He always sits straight up like there's a broomstick strapped to his back."

Cameron noticed his posture, and immediately leaned back in the couch.

"What the hell man, just say it," Isaac said. "Zoe, what's his problem?"

"I don't know," she said. "All I know is that right before they announced the recount, Cameron told the cameras to get ready on Glenda. He knew."

"You knew?" Isaac asked.

"Yes, he knew. He won't tell me how he knew, and he's been acting like a freaking cyborg ever since."

"How did you know?" Isaac asked.

Cam adjusted his glasses, and ran his hands through his hair. Then he stood up from the couch, to address both them. He turned, looked at his friend and girlfriend, and then plopped back down on the other end of the couch.

"It's nothing," he said.

"Oh my gosh dude, you know you're going to tell, just say it." Zoe demanded.

"No!"

"What is wrong with you, man?" Isaac asked.

"If I say it, then you two are going to rope me in on some wild goose chase, and it's going to consume the next two weeks of our lives, and I don't want to get into it. Because I don't care. I really don't."

"Don't care about what?" Isaac asked, looking back to the pool table, trying to coax the information out of Cameron's cracked armor.

"I don't care about the student council president. I think it's dumb."

"Why?" Zoe asked.

"Oh my gosh, cause we're in junior high. The student council president has basically no real power. Oh gee, should we wear uniforms or not wear uniforms? Who cares? Our parents already paid for the uniforms; you think they're going to let the school change that?"

Here he goes, Isaac thought. *It's coming.*

"Besides the uniforms, what other powers does the president actually have? I mean seriously? Like what do they do? They get to pick which grade gets the most field trips? Duh-eighth grade. It's always eighth grade. How does no one pay attention to this? It's the same with the votes. If I'm the only one who noticed the numbers were wrong, then what the heck do I care if the students in the school have Glenda or Moose as their president? It's all a distraction to keep us from realizing we're just kids and no one can actually stop us if we all showed up on the same day without uniforms. We could all just not wear them anymore, and there's nothing anyone can do about it. Am I the only one who sees that? But I don't care. I like wearing my uniform. The uniform keeps everyone equal. So I don't care."

"Okay, thank you James Madison," Zoe mocked. "Lots to digest there. What the heck was that supposed to mean?"

"The numbers were off?" Isaac asked. "What do you mean the numbers were off?"

"I didn't say that."

"Yes you did!" Zoe stood up. "Yes, he did. He just said the numbers were off." Zoe pointed an accusing finger at Cameron.

"What does that mean?" Isaac asked.

Cameron sprawled his body in the air like a used car lot balloon, "Who cares?"

Isaac walked around the couch with his pool stick in hand and pointed it in Cameron's face. "Listen,

Chen, it sounds to me like you got a real story here, and I want to know what the hell you're talking about."

"Me too," Zoe huffed crossing her arms.

Cameron waved the pool stick away from his face then rummaged his hands back and forth through his hair, knocking his glasses off-balance.

Geez, he's having a spazz attack, Isaac thought. *What does he not want to say?*

Cameron took a long deep inhale through his nose and exhaled then smeared his hands over his face again.

"Who's smarter?" Chen asked.

"What do you mean who's smarter?" Isaac asked.

"You know what I mean. Who do you actually think is smarter? Me or you?"

Isaac knew this was a rhetorical question, but it bothered him. Sure, Chen had better grades, and was probably better at math and science, but Isaac was no slouch. Isaac also had more social prowess. Of course, Cameron wanted Isaac to say Cameron's smarter. This is a test, and Isaac knows he should say Cameron. That's a big ask.

"If I say me, will you still tell me?" Isaac wished instantly he didn't say that.

"Forget it," Cameron flayed his hands in the air once more. He jumped off the couch to his feet, "Forget it!"

"Okay, dude. Come on. What do you want me to say? That I think you're smarter than me, Cameron?"

"This is so stupid," Zoe chimed in.

"No, I want you to say that you know I'm smarter," Chen said.

"Why?"

"Cause I stood by this election idea and it was stupid from the start," Cameron explained. "You couldn't be president, so you tried to *rig* the election? And you didn't even rig it; you just tried to find the dumbest kid possible to inflate your ego to see if he would win. And all because somehow this helps you have a better chance at getting a girl?"

Cameron turned to Zoe, "Which is really all your fault, you know?"

"Yes you've told me. For the record, I was pretty accurate considering she is now dating a high school—"

"—Doesn't matter! It's still dumb. This whole election, chasing Alyssa. All of it is so stupid."

"Just get to the damn point, will ya?" Isaac ask. "Okay, I'm dumb."

"Yeah," Zoe agreed. "We are dumb! So dumb. Stupid, immature, irresponsible, simple-minded, slow-witted, uneducated, unintelligent, ignorant, foolish, and naïve. Okay?"

"Fine," Cameron exhaled.

"But Isaac more so than me," Zoe clarified.

"When Jenny interviewed Mr. Stentson, he explained how the scantron machine reads the votes, do you remember that or were you too busy staring at Alyssa?"

"Dude, that's not fair. You know I don't pay attention to anything Jenny Towel does on camera."

Cameron pointed at Isaac with all five fingers to Zoe, "This is the puppet master?"

"Oh my gosh Cam, just say it. No one pays attention to Jenny, I wasn't paying attention. Jenny sucks."

Cameron sighed. *This is who runs my show with me?*

Zoe sat with her knees bent, both feet shaking subconsciously, literally at the edge of her seat in anticipation. Isaac gave off the same tense energy. Cameron knew he would tell them. He knew from the moment he noticed *it*. He just wanted to relish the attention.

Cameron built up this revealing statement in a crescendo. "While Mr. Stentson explained to Jenny how the scantrons worked, he said the machine scanned 'all 506 of them'!"

He ended with his eyes wide, mouth open, and hands out to his side. The response: nothing.

"So?" Isaac asked.

"You don't see the significance?" Cameron asked. He turned to Zoe, "Et tu Brute?"

"Ignoring whatever that means, and no," Zoe said. "I don't see it."

"How many eligible voters are there at Pine Lakes?"

"Well, technically no one is eligible, I'm pretty sure the votes were mandatory," Isaac responded.

"You guys, there are only 487 eligible-forced, mandatory, whatever, you want to call it, voters in school. 487."

Cameron let the statement sink for second. *Aahh that goes down like crisp cool soda, doesn't it?* Cameron felt dropping a big news story like that, totally blowing someone's mind with a fact, was as satisfying as a crisp cold fountain drink. He savored the flavor.

"How do you know the exact number of kids in school?" Isaac asked. "Why do you even know?"

"I check the ratings," Cameron explained.

"Dude. It's mandatory to watch the news, we don't have ratings," Zoe shouted.

The way Cameron's comment irritated Zoe to frustration so quickly, Isaac could tell this must be something they've argued about in the past, like a married couple.

"I check the attendance, I like to know how many people are watching everyday," Cameron snapped.

"But it's always going to basically be the same number. How many people can possibly be absent on the same day?"

"Okay guys, can we reel this back in?" Isaac asked.

"Because I check the ratings—"

"—Attendance!"

"—Whatever, because I check the attendance, I know there are 487 eligible voters: 168 sixth graders, 158 seventh graders, and 161 eighth graders. There couldn't be 506 votes."

Isaac scratched his head. Cameron was further ahead of him on this one that he could have imagined. He needed to make some quick mental leaps to get back in the race.

"So what's our angle?" Isaac asked, hoping to fast-forward through at least a few minutes of explanation that Cameron very obviously couldn't wait to divulge.

Isaac wasn't quite sure what the explanation actually was, hopefully Zoe would ask, or he'd piece it together as they moved forward. Cameron had enough limelight for one day.

"It's pretty simple," Cameron jabbed. "We have two options. First we can—"

"—Figure out if there was a mistake, or if it was intentional," Zoe blurted.

Cam raised his hands again, "Yes, and then find—"

"—Find out who did it," Isaac butt-in. "Chen, this is like a *real* story here."

"Docker's going to flip," Zoe said.

"No," Cameron and Isaac both said at the same time.

"We can't tell Docker," Chen insisted.

"Agreed," Isaac said. "I think he knows something's up."

"He's been acting weird," Zoe said. "What makes you two say that?"

"He wanted us off the recount thing, remember?" Isaac said.

"I concur, he's too close to this," Cameron said. He put his hand, motioning for the others to place their hand on top of his. "If we're really going after this one, and again for the record, I wanted it to let it be, but if we're doing it, we have to agree right now we're going dark. Real investigative journaling. We can't tell Docker or anyone else?"

In," Isaac said.

Zoe put her hand on top of the pile, "Sure, whatever."

They exchanged looks and then jerked their hands down quick and out and away from the center. The secret pact making process was complete.

CH 23

"Dude, you absolutely cannot freaking tell her," Cameron screeched his bike tires to a halt.

It was Friday. The plan was originally to go to Cameron's, as usual for the night, but Isaac mentioned he wanted to go to the local high school football game instead. It wasn't uncommon for junior high kids to go, if they liked sports. But why in the world did Isaac want to go? So he could hang out with Alyssa Sonoma of course, and he just finished telling Cameron he thought it would be a good idea to loop her into their secret investigative journaling pact.

"Why not?" Isaac asked.

"Dude Budgies, if you tell Alyssa that we found out the number of votes were wrong, how many freaking seconds do you think it will take her before she tells Macie and the rest of the school?"

"Those two aren't even really real friends," Isaac said.

"Isaac you are not thinking with your brain right now," Chen said. "There is zero chance you can tell her about this."

"Alright, think about it like this: there's you and Zoe behind the glass, and it's me and Alyssa up front. The four of us are a team; we need a fourth. She's the fourth."

"She's an idiot. And she's never been nice to me a day in her life. And she's dating a high schooler. Who she will be with at the game tonight, but you want to go creep in there and talk to her?"

"I think it would be fun, something different, you know?"

"Man, you are so hung up on this chick, it makes zero sense."

"Hey, do you want to go to the game or not?"

"No. Not at all."

"So, you just want me to go sit in your basement on another Friday night and listen to you and Zoe make-out with each other? Come on man. I'm sick of that; let's go to the game."

"You're not seeing the bigger picture here, Isaac. Just pick someone else. Anyone else. You're theoretically one of the most popular guys in school. Just find someone else."

"I don't want to," Isaac shouted. "We're going to the effing game tonight."

"Okay, wow. And you think I'm the spazz?"

🎥 🎥 🎥

"Oh my gosh, Mom, can you like please not pull all the way on to the touchdown?" Zoe begged from the passenger seat.

"Whoa, this is so cool," Mrs. Vernar said as they approached the high school turnaround. "I didn't realize so many younger kids come to these games too. You guys should do this more often."

"Yes, and see all the kids, Mom? They. Are. Walking. In. We don't need you to drive us up so close, oh my gosh."

"Oh look at all these little guys with their Pop Warner jerseys! Zoe, remember when you were a cheerleader?"

"Mom, I am literally dying, we need to get out of the car!"

"I agree, Mrs. Vernar," Cameron said from the backseat, "I think we can manage from here."

"Okay, okay. Good luck tonight, Isaac," Mrs. Vernar said. "I think it's so romantic of you stepping totally out of your element to go into enemy territory, where you are totally out numbered by big scary high school football guys, to try and get noticed by a girl who doesn't seem to notice you. I think it's so sweet."

Zoe turned around from the front to the guys in the backseat, "Sorry bud, we talk."

"What's wrong with that?" Mrs. Vernar asked. "I'm just saying I think it's so cool he's not embarrassed to come out here and take a gigantic chance like this."

"Getting there," Isaac faked a smile.

"Okay, Mom, the damage is done, will you let us out?"

Mrs. Vernar parked the car in the back lot, behind the home team stands. The snare drums from the marching band rattled off the metal bleachers. Car horns honked, families bickered as they headed toward the ticket counter, and the smell of popcorn and hot dogs hung in the air like a steamed fog. And there were the high school students *everywhere.* Teenage boys and girls in scarlet and grey, some with face-paint, or whacky pirate outfits to dress like the school's mascot, all clamoring to get inside before kickoff.

"I'm already bored," Zoe yawned.

"Oh c'mon," Isaac said. "This is kinda cool. It's okay to like sports."

"There's people here," Zoe replied.

"Okay, let's go casually bump into Alyssa and her boyfriend so we can get out of here," Cameron said.

The three of them wrestled their hands free through the crowd, pushing to get in, and turned over their tickets. They entered at the far end of the field with the concessions stand to the left, and very heavy foot traffic. The teams already took the field, but were still doing warm-ups. Isaac and company walked about ten feet through the metal gate fence when they heard, "Oh my gosh, you guys! What are you doing here?"

It was Glenda Howard.

Isaac felt a subtle dropping disappointed feeling in his gut, like thinking he found a quarter in his pocket, but it ended up being just a nickel.

"Oh. Hey Glenda," he said.

"I didn't know you were a sports fan," Cameron said, trying to break the tension.

"Oh I'm not," Glenda explained. "I'm here volunteering."

"Of course you are," Zoe eye rolled.

"Yeah, getting involved in the high school booster club, and community service groups is really important for me to start high school off on the right foot next year. I want to show Ivy League schools my volunteer work started prior to high school, while demonstrating a continued interest. It's all part of my five-year plan."

"We're here for work," Cameron said.

"So, where do the other kids from school sit?" Isaac asked, scanning the grandstand. He couldn't see her anywhere.

"Most of them sit in the top section on this end of the field," Glenda said. "See, there's some Pines

Lakers up there. But Alyssa usually sits with the high school student section."

"Alyssa who?" Isaac asked.

Zoe betrayed him with a laugh. Isaac wasn't fooling anyone.

"I thought since you guys are all here as a news team, maybe you wanted to sit with Alyssa Sonoma. But her and Macie are usually the only junior high kids I've ever seen in that section."

"And that's all the way on the far end of the field, huh?" Zoe asked. "So there's really no reason for us to walk down there if all the junior high kids sit right up here, right?"

"I can't think of any," Glenda answered.

Isaac bit his lip and scrunched his eyebrows shooting Zoe a glare.

"Okay, guys, let's go find a seat," Cameron suggested.

"Hey by the way," Glenda called as they turned. "No hard feelings."

"What do you mean?" Isaac asked.

"Yeah because even though you guys demanded a recount and basically implied that no one in school believed I could have won the majority vote, which did feel a bit like a personal attack, I want you to know it's no big deal. And I won't take that into account when I'm looking into the PLAN program's budget or possible considerations to shorten episodes," she smiled. "Go Pirates! Bye Isaac."

Once they were out of earshot, Zoe whispered, "Holy cow, that chick is power tripping. Did she just threaten us?"

"Relax," Cameron said, "Our episodes won't be shortened, and she doesn't have the power to set the budget."

"How do you know?" Zoe asked.

"Because she's thirteen years old!"

The three friends climbed the mountain of aluminum steps to the designated junior high students' area. Up in the nosebleeds and close to where the parents sat, they were definitely in the most *uncool* section of the stadium. But they did see some familiar faces, including Moose Patrowski and Jenny Towlel. Jenny nearly fell over the bleachers trying to greet them.

"Oh my gosh, oh my gosh! I feel like I'm out partying with my boss or something," she clapped. "What are you guys doing here?"

"Ask Isaac," Zoe suggested.

Jenny held out her notebook, "I thought it would be cool to start covering some more local sports in the morning. I was actually going to bring it up on Monday. Pretty good idea, right Isaac?"

"First good idea I've heard in a few days," Cameron said.

"Do you guys want to sit with me? I mean probably not right? You're probably going to sit with the eighth graders."

"Where do the eight graders sit?" Isaac asked.

"Well everyone from Pine Lakes pretty much sits right here, I just meant—you know—like in a different row or something. Except I don't really see too many eighth graders tonight. Just Moose and some basketball guys."

"I guess here is fine," Isaac dropped to his seat with a thump. Jenny sat two rows in front of them, but sat turned to keep the conversation going.

"Did you guys see that Alyssa is here too? I think it's so dumb she sits with the high school kids though," Jenny added. Trying to do anything she could to take her competition down a notch in Isaac's eyes. "I'm pretty sure the other high school kids don't even want her around. I mean like think about it: if you were in high school why would you want to be talking to some younger kid, you know?"

"Oh I know," Zoe said, raising her eyebrows to Jenny.

Don't even bother, Zoe told herself. *No chance Jenny has that kind of self awareness.*

Isaac checked out of the conversation. His eyes went off into a stare and the wheels in his head started churning. He imagined math equations and vectors and angles and speed formulas. He envisioned the triangles of the steps, the area of the stadium walkway compared to the length of his legs and size of his shoes, and the width of his field of vision.

"What's the plan?" Cameron asked.

"Well, no chance I'd be caught dead walking all the way to the far end of the stadium with no reason to be there, right?"

"Not unless you wanted to look super desperate," Zoe confirmed.

Jenny Towlel sat with her head cocked giving a full ear of attention to the eighth grade news team.

"My only chance is she'll have to eat something. Right? I'll see her coming from her section, and I'll just time it out to walk down there and intercept her path."

"For a guy with so much pride, you certainly have no shame," Zoe said.

"It's a simple enough plan," Cameron said. "So, instead of coming here to watch the game, we're going to watch the foot traffic in the stadium? Exciting."

CH 24

Isaac hardly watched a single play of the game. Every time the team scored a touchdown, it was harder for him to keep his eye on the stadium lanes because everyone jumped up and down, and then remained standing while the band played their fight song. On top of that, practically everyone was wearing red, and Isaac had no idea what Alyssa was wearing. After the first quarter, Isaac thought it would be even smarter to hang out at the concession stand and just wait for her to show up. Zoe convinced him that would be too creepy and he should just be patient.

Then he saw her at halftime. Halftime: the busiest and worst time of a football game to try and get snack. Alyssa was making her way from the far end of the stands towards the concession booths.

"That's gotta burn a little, huh?" Zoe asked.

She didn't clarify, but Isaac correctly assumed the *burn* Zoe referred to was Alyssa walking towards them very clearly wearing a freshman football player's jersey. But Isaac didn't see the white jersey with red numbers and red and black stripes. To him, it was a moving dartboard, and Isaac needed to hit a bull's-eye. He ignored Zoe and stood up.

"Oh are you going to get something to eat?" Jenny asked. "I'll come with you."

Not taking no for an answer, Jenny stood up with her purse and clamped down the aluminum steps in stride with Isaac.

What is she doing? He wondered. *She's going to ruin everything.*

Zoe and Cameron exchanged looks and smirks, then smiles, and finally after the two others were far enough away, they laughed at Isaac.

"She's going to blow it," Zoe cackled.

Those b–words, Alyssa Sonoma thought to herself. *Do not cry*, she tried using her tongue to push out her lower jaw as wide as possible. *What did they know anyways? Stupid high school girls. And like what the hell? Why didn't my boyfriend stick up for me? Like, he just sat there the whole time and he practically laughed. And is he following me? Like why hasn't he chased me down yet? Am I walking too fast? Walk slower.*

The sharp tingle in the corner of her eyelids crept back into her senses. *No! No Alyssa, absolutely not*. She would not let herself cry in public. She could fake cry whenever she wanted, but she dared not show her real emotions and cry in public. *Oh my gosh can you imagine how embarrassing that would be?*

Alyssa imagined: she'd be standing right there in the same spot she was in, but she'd be crying. And those cheerleaders down on the field would see her and point to each other and start laughing. Then the crowd would see the cheerleaders laughing—because everyone is always watching the cheerleaders—and people would start to notice what the cheerleaders were looking at and they'd point and laugh at her too.

Oh my gosh, why hasn't he followed me? High school boys are so stupid. And I'm sure those high school snobs would eat that up too, that my boyfriend didn't even chase after me. Like has he ever seen a movie? Oh my gosh don't cry.

Her imagination continued. The cheerleaders would hold up signs that said, "Alyssa Sonoma doesn't even go to this school." And they'd make fun of her even more.

And okay, so what if my mom dropped me off? Um, lots of people get dropped off by their own parents. Lots of people in eighth grade anyways.

And then the band would see that her make-up was running and they'd start playing a song while pointing at her. Then the referees would even blow the whistle and stop the game just so that everyone in the whole freaking stadium could watch her crying and leaving by herself. Gosh Alyssa hated those older girls. They made her feel so small and immature for still being in junior high. They didn't want her sitting with them.

They weren't even that cute either! No. She said to herself. *Do not cry. He isn't going to follow you either. This is the worst day of my life. Ew and I am still wearing his freaking jersey! I want to scream and explode.*

Meanwhile, in Isaac's mind: the field disappeared. He was not in the stadium anymore. The green grass from the football field spread over the railings, covered the stadium and everyone in it, and grew to tall trees. He was in the jungle now. He was a panther, stalking a small deer in the shadows of the forest floor with his eyes, nose, and ears on her. The deer hadn't seen him yet. *Oh man she is so freaking hot, look at her hair. How does Cameron not get it? I'm in eighth grade; my hormones are as volatile right now as a Uranium isotope, okay? I'm allowed to have a crush on whoever I want.*

This is practically a date, Jenny jeered to herself. *If he buys me this hotdog, it's a date! Oh my gosh, I am on a date with Isaac Budgies right now. At the football game with Isaac Budgies, and he is going to buy me something at the concession stands. I feel like I am in a movie. Am I talking out loud? Gosh he's walking so fast down these steps.*

In a quiet British narrator's voice Isaac narrated for himself: *"It is important for the panther not to pounce too soon. The young eighth grade girl is easily startled in the wild. In almost impossible odds, she's managed to stray away from her herd. His timing will have to be perfect."*

"What are you going to order?"

SNAP!

Isaac's entire imagination disintegrated. He was back in reality midway down the stadium steps. He nearly fell over when he realized Jenny was still following him. He half-turned over his shoulder to acknowledge her but didn't stop his stride.

"I don't know."

"I cant decide if I want nachos or something bigger. Nachos are good to share but sometimes . . ."

Isaac focused in on Alyssa.

". . . Eye-zick?" Jenny broke through again. "Didn't you hear me?"

"Oh yeah, me too," he said.

The narrator's voice came back over his mind: *"Unexpectedly, a young howler monkey has approached creating a raucous, pestering the hunter."*

"But you don't think that's too much food?" Jenny asked.

"Just hold on a second," Isaac said, not even turning around. He let a couple walk in front of him on the aisle. This should give him a buffer with his time of approach.

In just a few more seconds, Isaac would intercept Alyssa perfectly in stride. He was going to look so cool. This is one of those things he wished he had on camera, like throwing something into a garbage can from really far away on the first try.

Oh no, Jenny finally saw her. Alyssa Sonoma would not ruin her first date with Isaac Budgies. Jenny cocked her chin up and tugged on Isaac's sleeve.

What the heck is she doing? Jenny Towlel is not going to screw this up for me. Ignore her.

They approached the final step. Alyssa walked with eyes straight ahead, so concentrated, she hadn't noticed Isaac. Isaac was so concentrated on getting his timing perfect, he didn't notice she was holding back tears. He dropped from off the last step.

"Hey Alyssa!" Jenny and Isaac said at the exact same time, sending chills and regret through Isaac's entire body.

CH 25

"Dude, you freaking told her?" Cameron gasped in the parking lot.

The game ended, students hustled about looking for rides and shouting out plans, others took photos celebrating the win. Zoe didn't know who won. Her fun was just starting while Cameron and Isaac argued in the parking lot.

"You swore you wouldn't tell her," Cameron went on, "I was there, remember? We all put our hands into a circle, looked at each other in the eyes, and we promised each other we wouldn't tell anyone about this? I'm even pretty sure I specifically said 'don't tell Alyssa.'"

"You definitely didn't say that," Isaac rebutted.

"Doesn't matter, Isaac. Doesn't matter. She still falls under the umbrella of *anyone*!"

"So um—should I not be standing right here?" Jenny Towlel asked. They were the only four people waiting in the bus turnaround for a pickup. Jenny stood an awkward six feet away from the three others. Originally, she thought they'd invite her to some sort of hang out session after the game, probably not a sleepover, but maybe.

"Jenny, this is a private conversation," Cameron answered.

"Just leave her," Isaac mumbled. "She was there too."

"Ohrg-ha!" Zoe reacted.

"What?" Cameron asked.

"Yeah," Isaac shrugged. "She knows too."

"Jenny Towlel? Dude, you told Jenny, the seventh grade cafeteria correspondent, Towlel? Our secret? The one that nobody else was supposed to know?"

"She wouldn't leave me alone, man what was I supposed to do?" Isaac was getting louder now. "I have Alyssa practically in tears blah-blahing to me about something about her boyfriend and the high school girls giving her a hard time, and—"

"—And so you told her our top secret news story in an attempt to garner attraction from her? Meanwhile, saying it in front of Jenny Towlel because you are that selfish?"

"Still here guys," Jenny smiled.

"Alright first of all, Jenny's fine," Isaac defended himself by defending her.

He thinks I'm fine? Oh my gosh, like fine like okay fine or like hot fine? This is exciting! We are going to be dating after tonight. Probably already would be if that crybaby Alyssa didn't cockblock me.

"Jenny gets it, this is news. This is confidential. It's totally off the record. She isn't going to say anything to anyone."

"Well that's what you promised to me—"

"Us," Zoe corrected, not because she cared but because she liked fast interjections when Cameron rambled.

"—Right. Promised to us. Before you told Alyssa."

"Okay, so I'm like just going to take ten steps this way, and put in my headphones okay?" Jenny asked.

"Unbelievable dude," Cameron said.

"Sorry last thing, my ride is going to be here soon, Isaac how do you want to get my number? Or should I just message you? I have yours."

Zoe laughed out loud.

"Um, I'll just see you at school on Monday."

CH 26

Moose Patrowski walked through the halls with his backpack slung over one shoulder and his pelvic thrust out far in front of his feet. He swung his free arm all the way forward and back so as to be ready to give out high-fives or thumbs-ups wherever needed. It was not often needed, but if Moose got one high-five in a day, it felt to him that he'd gotten a hundred in the week. Inaudible music played only for Moose to hear inside his mind. Moose often felt a genuine level of sincere and honest sympathy for every student at Pine Lakes who wasn't fortunate enough to be Moose Patrowski. He pitied people who didn't have such an amazing life as him. This will lead to several confrontations and a myriad of issues later on in Moose's life, but for now he was a harmless narcissist. Losing the election meant nothing to him.

"Oh there you are Mr. Patrowski," Ms. Lungar said in the hallway, interrupting his morning stroll.

"Hey, I didn't even go to that party," Moose responded.

Ms. Lungar scribbled on her notebook to remind herself to investigate something later, and said, "No. I am not here to discipline you, Mr. Patrowski. I'm just reminding you that there will be an introductory student council meeting tomorrow morning."

"I have basketball practice after school," Moose said. This was his go-to excuse. He used it so often, and it always worked, that whenever he heard any adult say anything regarding any sort of time commitment, the words just came out of his mouth.

"That won't be a problem, the meeting is before school," Ms. Lungar clarified.

"But why do I have to go? I didn't win the election, which is like total B.S."

"Language, Mr. Patrowski. And just because you didn't win the election, I presume you maintain an interest in the student council. A desire to be involved in the school's community, do you not?"

Moose struggled to find the words to most delicately convey to Ms. Lungar that indeed, he had absolutely no desire to do anything involving or associated with dorks and/or school related activities, outside of sports and possibly a school play.

"Well, I mean, like, if they didn't even vote for me, then why should I even go?"

"Mr. Patrowski, as a finalist for the presidential seat, it is presumed that you act as your classroom's representative on the student council. I'm sure at some other schools in the area, Student Council may be a monthly casual commitment, but not here at Pine Lakes. I will remind you, that a seat on the Pine Lakes' Student Council, is reserved for those who will not sit back. The school year is quite young, we have plenty of opportunities for you to make a difference."

"Like how ... how many opportunities?"

"We meet every week for one hour on Tuesday mornings. Then twice a month, we will have a lunch meeting. Of course, you'll be expected to volunteer for at least two after school functions a month as well. For example: concessions stands for a girls basketball game, or on a Saturday when the school hosts the local Farmer's market."

Moose's neck went hot and his skin itched. *Mornings? Saturdays? Is this lady nuts?* He didn't want to do any of that kind of crap on his time off. *She's out of her mind. No way.*

"But I'm not the student body president," Moose said. *Is she confused or something?*

"Well of course not," Ms. Lungar laughed. "Glenda's responsibilities will be far more demanding. Her and I have already discussed the notion of forming an Advisory Board. We think this would be another opportunity for volunteerism and community outreach. Would you like me to add your name to the shortlist of candidates?"

Ms. Lungar clicked down on her pen to begin writing again.

"No!" Moose lunged forward. "I mean, um, no thanks. I think, um, there's probably a lot of demand for that sort of, like, I don't know. If other kids want to do that, let them have it."

"Cold feet? Or just lack of commitment?"

"That just seems like a lot of my time right now."

"But you're the one who ran for school president. I thought you wanted to get involved?"

"Yeah but I didn't win, so I just kind of . . ."

"Moose, if you're going to involve yourself in the world of student politics, you'll need to understand volunteering your time is critical."

"Yeah but like, I think I want to ease into it a little, you know?"

"You don't ease yourself into academic politics, Moose. It's like a hot pepper: you bite off more than you can chew right from the start and you sweat it out."

The school bell rang.

"Okay, I have to go," Moose said.

"Just a second," Ms. Lungar said. Then she tore off a piece of her notebook and handed it to Moose.

"A tardy slip? Are you kidding me? You were talking to me!"

"No one is above the rules, Mr. Patrowski."

"Come on, for real?"

"I'm sorry there's nothing I can do about it. Rules are rules, and you're late for class."

"Whatever," Moose said after he tuned to walk away.

He thought about how much time he just saved himself by losing the election. He made a mental reminder to confront that Isaac Budgies smartass about not telling him anything about *volunteering*. If Moose knew he was going to have to do that he would have saved himself the trouble from the get-go. *Only dorks do that kind of stuff.*

"Punk." Of course, Ms. Lungar didn't say that out loud, but she thought it. And maybe she even "Mmphed," audibly a little bit, but she wasn't quite sure.

I hate children, she thought.

CH 27

"Why the heck do you want to do that?" Cameron asked Glenda.

"Well, I just think it would be cool, you know? Like a personal montage for myself; for everyone."

"Listen, Glenda," Cameron started. He pinched his nose to begin the sentence. "We don't have the bandwidth to assign someone to cut that material."

Cameron wanted to find an excuse for why he was too busy. But he couldn't say he was in the middle of orchestrating a sting operation to uncover a deep conspiracy, the likes of which have never before been known to Pine Lakes Academy. He stumbled to find words, his hands looked for them at the back of his neck.

"I mean, I've got a sixth grade shadow, to whom I need to start focusing on to turning over creative duties. Isaac is really focused on, uh, and Zoe is —"

"—I'll do it," Zoe said.

"Great!" Glenda smiled and walked away.

"Zoe, what are you doing?" Cameron asked.

As Glenda walked away, Isaac strolled up. He seemed particularly proud of himself this Monday morning. He was wearing new shoes; Zoe and Cameron both noticed instantly, but they wouldn't say anything.

"What's going on over here?" Isaac asked. "You guys didn't say anything to Glenda about the—"

"—Of course not," Cameron answered. "You did enough damage with roping Jenny Towlel into the mix."

"Hey, we can trust Jenny," Isaac whispered.

"Shh, shut up," Cameron motioned. "We can't talk about this here; it's not safe."

Isaac raised his eyebrows to Zoe, mocking Cameron.

"She just signed us up for a PR stunt for Glenda," Cameron said half pointing at Zoe while flaying his hand to the sky.

"I actually think it's a good idea," Zoe said.

"We don't have the time."

"Look, your student body president just asked you to turnover some election B-roll to the Yearbook committee, what is so hard with that?"

"That's all evidence!" Cameron pulled his hair. "We need that footage, I haven't had time to go through it yet."

"Oh my gosh, Captain," Zoe rolled her eyes. "Evidence of what? A deep cover-up of junior high school's student council presidential election scandal?"

"Yes. Yes, exactly that."

"I'll start going through the film today after school," Zoe said.

"I'll help," Isaac added.

"You'll help?" Zoe asked. "Are you like sick or something?"

"I need an excuse to stay after school, okay?"

Zoe crossed her arms.

"I don't want Jenny Towlel finding me at the bike racks. I'm running out of excuses to avoid her."

"You always have a self-serving reason."

"And why are you doing it?"

"Cause Cameron doesn't want me to," she winked.

"Well, now I have to come too," Cameron said.

"What? You don't trust me alone with your girlfriend?"

"Of course not, but that's besides the point. I don't trust you two alone with my *film*," Cameron said.

Zoe punched Cam's arm.

🎥 🎥 🎥

"This is hard to watch," Zoe said.

The three of them sat in the editing room, the clock on the wall read *4:27*, and they were going to be there for a while longer it seemed. Finding the right B-roll, which is extra footage, to turnover to the yearbook committee wasn't as easy a task as Zoe thought. The three of them knew the politics involved with yearbooking. First and foremost, it should be mostly centered on the eighth graders, and they didn't have their footage labeled as properly as Cameron would have liked. It took quite a bit of fast-forwarding through classroom voting sessions to find the eighth grade homerooms.

Finally, they came across the recordings from Isaac and Alyssa's camera. Zoe made a snarky comment about Alyssa's camerawork. They were all staring at a shot of Isaac doing a quick introduction and explanation that they'd be heading inside to watch Mrs. Bescomb's sixth grade homeroom's voting procedure.

Isaac refused they fast-forward through anything with him on camera, so they sat to re-watch his report.

"You're all over the frame," Cameron said. "Look at this, she's shaking the camera."

"Did she film this on a rollercoaster?" Zoe asked.

Isaac tried to ignore them. He mostly focused on how he looked on screen. He wouldn't say anything bad about Alyssa, at least at first. But then, when he saw she was visible through the reflection of the classroom window Isaac stood in front of, she was hard to defend.

A basic camera operator should have at least known not to be caught on her own camera. Standing there, over Isaac's shoulder with the transparent image of the camera over her shoulder, it was so distracting. Isaac couldn't argue at all about why Cameron previously chose to cut this sequence from the broadcast.

"How could she not even have seen that?" Zoe asked. "Do you think she just wanted to be in the frame too? It's like a visual Freudian slip."

"Okay, that's pretty bad," Isaac admitted.

"I just don't get your obsession with her," Zoe said.

"Let's not go over this again, okay?"

"I'm telling you, it's an ego thing," Cameron said. "You like her because she ignores you. That's all it is. If she chased after you the way Jenny Towlel does, you wouldn't think twice about her."

Isaac allowed himself to daydream:

Budgies pictures himself walking down the school hallway. The bustling students part like the Red Sea so that he can pass without interference. He's in slow motion, his uniform pressed perfectly, looking brand new, not a wrinkle in sight. Every girl in school smiles and waives hello saying his name. Athletes give him high fives and hall monitors give him blank hall passes with a wink. Then Alyssa Sonoma turns the corner and her eyes focus on his. She licks her lips and approaches.

"Oh Isaac," Alyssa says in his daydream. "I'm obsessed with you. Will come over to my house after school and make-out with me?"

"Oh my gosh!" Zoe shrieked.

The interruption bolts Isaac back to reality.

"She doesn't even know how to stop a recording, Isaac," Zoe sighed. "I mean come on, I get that we're hard on the girl but look at this. You're walking out of the room and she's still got the camera running. What a waste of film."

"Stop! What was that?" Cameron asked. He flung his hand across the desk grabbing the computer mouse out of the Zoe's hand.

"Spazz much?"

"Just wait a second," he said.

Cameron had his nose about one inch away from the computer monitor as he dragged the footage backward. The monitor reflected off his lenses.

On screen, Isaac smiled into the camera and paused there for a count, waiting for Alyssa to give him a queue she stopped recording but it never came. As the camera lowered when Alyssa took it off her shoulder, it kept recording.

"There. Did you see it?" Cameron asked. "Stop looking at yourself Isaac and watch it again."

Cameron dragged the footage back again. Isaac ignored himself this time and watched through the window, through Alyssa's reflection and into the classroom.

"No way," Zoe's mouth dropped.

"Play it again," Isaac said.

Cameron rewound and replayed the footage again.

"Aaaand right there!" Cameron said pointing to the monitor, he paused the screen. "She puts it in the envelope!"

"I can't believe what I'm seeing," Zoe said.

"I can't believe Alyssa, of all people, got it on camera," Cameron admitted.

Isaac didn't say anything. He couldn't believe his eyes. Clear as day, Mrs. Bescomb filled out a scantron herself and put it inside the envelope. Cameron paused the footage, although slightly blurry, there was an irrefutable shot of Mrs. Bescomb sliding her own scantron into the voting envelop along with the rest of them from her class.

"The teachers aren't supposed to vote," Isaac finally said.

"It *was* rigged," Cameron said.

"This is like, for real, a news story," Zoe said.

"So cool," Jenny Towlel chimed in from the doorway. Causing the other three to jump in their seats.

"Oh no," Cameron slapped his forehead.

CH 28

"Okay, the reason we are all here is because we need to expose why the number of votes was wrong," Cameron explained to Isaac, Zoe, Alyssa, and Jenny sitting together at a lunch table. Jenny looked particularly proud of herself sitting in the raised section reserved normally for eighth graders only. "And because Isaac has a big mouth."

Isaac couldn't help but share the news with Alyssa about discovering the tape. Breaking an actual news story, doing real investigative journalism, like a stakeout, with Alyssa sounded to Isaac like a great date. He told her within an hour of promising Cameron he wouldn't. *Jenny already knew*, he reasoned. *Can't hurt too much to tell Alyssa.*

Alyssa was hardly present at this secret meeting, being held in the very public setting of the school cafeteria. Her eyes bounced around the lunchroom taking notes of every glance, stare, glare, smirk, and smile of those watching her sit at the table, with those people, again! People would think she probably had a falling out with Macie.

They're probably all thinking the rumors are true. That I personally sabotaged Macie's campaign, she thought.

After the election results came out, Macie had an even harder time than Moose accepting the reality of the vote. In fact, Macie blamed it entirely on Alyssa. The pre-recorded talk show session that aired only days before the election made Moose look comical and funny. Worse, the video also made Macie look shallow and rude. The truth was Macie made herself look shallow and rude. Macie believed it was the video that lost her foothold in the polls. She insisted that somehow Alyssa deliberately was out to destroy her. All of this was true, of course, but the rumors were tarnishing Alyssa's reputation. Alyssa hoped to prove the rumors false, in that she didn't deliberately set out for Macie to lose the election. She hoped for that result secretly.

Like, who would even start that rumor? Probably Macie. I mean, I've started worse rumors about her.

"Okay Alyssa?" Cameron asked.

"Sorry, what?"

"I just went through the whole plan," Cameron's hair reached for the sky. "Did you hear anything I just said?"

"I didn't realize you were talking to me," she shrugged.

"I was addressing the group as whole," Cameron groaned. Cameron turned to Isaac for support, rolling his eyes. "I'm not going to repeat all that again."

"Look, what's the deal?" Alyssa asked, blunt and direct.

"We think the teachers rigged the election and as I just said, the only way to prove it is to somehow get our hands on those voter slips."

"Okay. Easy," Alyssa shrugged.

Cameron closed his eyes, took a deep breath in through his nose, and exhaled loud and painfully while opening his eyes back to Alyssa. He exchanged a quick glance to communicate with Zoe.

With the most minor of fluctuations of the small muscles in her cheeks, forehead, slightly around her eyes, and a hair's width flare of her nostrils, Zoe signaled for Cameron to be patient.

"What do you mean easy?" Jenny asked. "Cameron just said it. We don't even know where they are. Like what if —"

Alyssa interrupted while Jenny tried talking about what if the scantrons were somehow thrown away, or something like that. However, Jenny didn't get to finish her thought because Alyssa interrupted her with a cold monotone, almost reptilian calmness. Like a veteran. Alyssa must have spent years studying the psychology of popularity. She leaned into the table, towards Zoe, Isaac, and Cameron, never for an instant acknowledging or noticing that Jenny was trying to speak. The way Alyssa leaned in with her interruption, actually lowering her voice, not raising it, somehow pulled in the attention of the other three off of Jenny.

"I'll just sneak into the teacher's lounge and find them."

Isaac, who was already staring at Alyssa while she spoke, raised his eyes to hers in shock.

"What? How are you going to do that?" Jenny asked as surprised as the rest of them. She interrupted herself to ask the question.

"Um, quick and quiet. Duh," Alyssa said. What she didn't mention to the rest of the group was Alyssa's personal motivation to prove something else: if someone else affected the outcome of the election, it would get her off the hook with Macie.

Alyssa imagined the Pine Lakes Academy News announcement going live into every televised classroom in the building and clearing her name. She'd prove to everyone that Macie Neadle not only lost the election, but she's actually a huge lying snob? *This could put me over Macie on the food chain permanently. Worth the risk.*

Isaac needed to decide how to play his response. Typically, he liked to pretend he had a *bad boy* persona, so to speak. Yet, Isaac wasn't one to do anything that would risk him getting into any actual trouble. Isaac questioned authority sure, but he wasn't as much of a rebel as he led on to be. He couldn't risk anything that would get his on-air privileges taken away. On the other hand, Alyssa liked older guys, it made sense she'd also be attracted to a risk-taker. His heart fluttered inside himself while he was about to conspire to trespassing into the teacher's lounge. This was big time.

"I don't think that's a good idea," Cameron said.

"Why not? Do you like have a better idea? You said you can't prove anything without the scantrons right?"

Cameron deferred to Zoe.

"Is there any other way to get the scantrons?" Zoe asked.

"Couldn't we just like ask Principal Lungar for them?" Jenny asked.

Alyssa, Zoe, Isaac, and Cameron all looked at Jenny, acknowledging that she said something, but then turned back to themselves to completely dismiss her suggestion. Cameron didn't even want to waste his breath explaining the absurdity of accusing the teachers of being involved in a voting conspiracy, and then asking them for the evidence.

"I'll help you," Isaac volunteered.

Of course he will, Zoe thought to herself, pitying her friend. Isaac Budgies: golden boy in the eyes of the school administration, would risk getting into serious trouble, perhaps a suspension or worse, to sneak into the school after hours, just to try and get Alyssa alone with him in a dark room? *Boys are dumb.*

"No thanks," Alyssa said to Isaac.

"My student ID card gets us into the teachers lounge. I can help," Isaac insisted. "That's also top secret," he said to Jenny.

Cameron wondered if Isaac already forgot why it was they needed to sneak into the lounge in the first place. He was spilling secrets left and right too. *This isn't a date, dude,* he wanted to tell him.

"I'll come too," Jenny chimed in, not liking the idea of her true love being alone with a floozy like Alyssa.

"No," the four others replied in unison.

"Too many people is too risky," Zoe said nicely.

CH 29

"Okay, let's go through the supplies one more time," Cameron said.

Three walkie-talkies, three flashlights, student IDs, keys, bicycle helmets, cell phones, water bottles, black sweat shirts, and a line of rope sat on Cameron's pool table.

"Not sure we needed the rope," Isaac said. Isaac inspected the neon yellow line of rope Cameron's dad had leftover from a water skiing line.

"No, probably not, but feels authentic, you know?"

"Yeah, let's bring it."

"What are we going to find? Over." Isaac said into his walkie-talkie as they loaded up the backpack.

"We're trying to find proof the teachers voted, over." Cameron responded in his walkie-talkie as well.

"And then what? Over."

"I'm not sure yet, Over." Cameron said. "Okay, let's go get her."

"Still don't think you need to come babysitting me though," Isaac said, grateful Cameron actually volunteered himself to come with as an additional watch. Cameron's reasoning was that it was his story to produce, and that if something went wrong, the captain always goes down with his ship. Isaac didn't put up much of a fight because if he was going to get in trouble, he might as well have Cameron get in trouble too. Both of them getting caught wouldn't look nearly as bad in the press. Also, if both Isaac and Cameron were caught, there might not be any press to report it. Plus, if Cameron was there to look for the documents, he might be able to finally make-out with Alyssa.

🎥 🎥 🎥

"I can't believe I'm doing this," Isaac said.

Cameron and Isaac rode their bikes into the dusk down the street towards Alyssa's house. She lived in the nicest neighborhood in town, but Isaac always found it odd they couldn't afford street lights in her subdivision. Huge houses, big winding driveways, but not a speck of light on the street.

"Look man," Cameron said, "If we get caught in there, we can get into some serious trouble, it has to be in and out."

"Yeah, sure. I just meant, I can't believe I'm actually going to the Sonoma's house. Haven't been here since third—"

"—Dude!" Cameron said. "Are you taking this seriously at all? We are about to uncover teachers cheating, and a conspiracy inside the faculty. All you're thinking about is Alyssa?"

Isaac played the scenario out in his head all day. In fact, the only two things on his mind for the rest of that afternoon were how he'd make-out with Alyssa in the teacher's lounge, and that he better not get called on to stand up in front of the class.

"This is pretty high stakes right now," Cameron said. "It's not a game."

Isaac parked his bike and took a deep breath before he approached her front door.

"What I can't figure out is why Alyssa is so concerned about this," Cameron said. "I've been trying to put my finger on it all day."

"I think she's trying to quash the rumors that she tried to get Macie to lose on purpose. So if the teachers rigged the election, this clears her."

"But she's taking a big risk to figure that, don't you think?"

"Well she wants to break the story," Isaac said. "And she figures if she's the one who walks through the door first, she gets to be the one to say it."

What Isaac didn't say, which Cameron knew was implied, is that Isaac's own personal ego wanted to be the one to share the news with the school.

"She is crazy. You just don't want to see it."

"Maybe she's just a good reporter, can't you see that?"

"No one watching her sees that. Just go ring the doorbell."

As Isaac walked to the front door, he imagined how many different ways the scenario could unfold. Would it be her mom who answers? Step-dad? Or maybe her housekeeper? Isaac replayed how he'd handle each situation, each different greeting, until he reached only a few steps away from the front door.

Maybe Alyssa would answer the door. Maybe she'd say her parents weren't home, invite him inside, and then—

"—I'm over here," Alyssa said from her electric scooter on the street next to Cameron. "Don't ring the doorbell, my mom has friends over."

Isaac sauntered back to them, wondering how Alyssa came out of the garage without him even hearing her. He knew he zoned out, but was embarrassed by how inattentive he had been.

"Ready to go break into the teacher's lounge?" Alyssa asked him. "Kinda expected it to be like darker you know?"

"I can't be out later than 9:00 on a school night," Cameron explained.

"There's no afterschool events tonight. The building should be empty by now," Isaac explained. "It's dark enough."

CH 30

Pine Lakes Academy sits atop a hill, facing east. The sun already started to set, casting a grey hue across the sky. It was just dark enough that Isaac felt using a flashlight was uncool. They could still see the school's front door from down the street.

"Which door do we go in?" Cameron asked.

"I left the window in the girls bathroom stall unlocked," Alyssa said. "Should be able to get in through there."

"Diabolical," Cameron whispered. "Let's go one street over and leave our bikes at the park. We can hop the fence from there."

Isaac's heart was racing so fast his smart watch beeped and asked him if he wanted to record a workout. He gripped his handlebars tighter to prevent the sensation of his shaking hands. He squeezed but felt no matter how hard he tried, he couldn't get a good grip from his nerves. To calm himself down, he tried to focus on breaking into the school and less on making out with Alyssa.

The large public park backed up to the school ground's furthest fence. It wasn't unheard of for kids to jump the fence in the summer and play in the school's large open field. Likely, anyone driving by at night seeing three figures walking across the field would not think much of it, unless that person was a police officer, teacher, or a concerned parent. Isaac jumped the fence first, then Cameron.

The second Alyssa put one foot up on the fence, her phone chirped.

"You didn't silence your phone?" Cameron asked. "I said it like four times."

Alyssa pulled her phone from her pocket and Isaac undeniably saw the bright screen reading: "♥♥JOHN♥♥"

Oh this is effing perfect timing, Isaac thought to himself.

Alyssa stopped thinking. She lowered her foot off the fence to read the text. She replied at about 200 WPM. Her thumbs tapped in a rapid fire blur as if they were animated by special effects.

"We're sort of in the middle of something here," Isaac said. Did he sound jealous or petty? *Well, who cares?* He was both.

Another chirp.

Alyssa smiled, "Sorry. It's my mom." She then replied with another display of rattling thumbs, which created a string of letters, backspaces, and emojis.

Cameron looked to Isaac. Cameron clenched his jaw, moved it from one side to the other, and raised each of his eyebrows from right to left. Isaac interpreted this body language to be saying, "Dude, are you still going to be cool going if she bails?"

Isaac grunted.

"Are you coming or not?" He said through the chain link fence separating Alyssa from both Cameron and Isaac.

Alyssa, too busy hammering away texts on her phone, took much too long to reply.

"Sorry, I can't. My mom wants me home," she lied. She also smiled and giggled at the texts she was getting.

"You realize if we find something in there it's going to be Isaac's story to tell?" Cameron asked.

Isaac was impressed. The question could be interpreted as Cameron trying to convince Alyssa to come. And it worked. She bit her lower lip and looked up at the height of the fence.

"Don't you want to report a real story?" Isaac asked, doing as much as he could to cover his desperation. Giving his best effort to convince himself he was there for a story, and not for the girl behind the fence.

Her phone chirped again.

"Honestly guys, I have bigger news going on right now," she said, defying the laws of physics by reaching her hand through the metal links of the fence and stabbing Isaac in the heart. Not actually, but that's what Isaac felt just happened.

"Nobody in high school cares about this kinda stuff," she said.

Isaac saw a giant metal Middle-Finger drop on his head and explode on him.

"I got to go," she said. "Good luck." And she turned away. Never lifting her eyes off from her phone. Her thumbnails clicked away like a pack of dogs walking on a hardwood floor.

"Forget her dude," Cameron said. "Let's go."

Isaac didn't reply. What could he say? That the most recent love of his life just bailed on him at the threshold of one of the most rebellious things he would ever attempt? *For bigger news? What could be bigger news?*

"I feel like I just got left at the altar," Isaac mumbled. He kept one hand hooked on the fence.

"I don't see what you see in her," Cameron said.

Well aware that they could get into a lot of trouble, Isaac responded by yelling at Cameron while also simultaneously whispering.

"I don't care if you don't see it, okay? I like her!"

"Okay, look. Let's talk about it later?" Cameron motioned for Isaac to walk away from the fence. "Can we please go uncover a gigantic voting conspiracy? It's getting late."

Isaac took his hand off the fence. *Gosh, she always does this to me,* he thought.

"She always does this stuff, man," Cameron said.

Why does she like getting my hopes up? Isaac asked himself.

"Some chicks just like getting guys' hopes up." Cameron said. "She'll be like that her whole life. Let's go do our jobs."

He's right, Isaac thought to himself. "You're right," he said aloud to Cameron. "She's not worth it."

Cameron hoped it was too dark for Isaac to see he was smiling, *Finally!* Cameron said to himself.

"Forget her, man. Let's go break into the school."

CH 31

"I'm pretty nervous," Cameron admitted. "Breaking into the school? I mean, is this us? Is this the stuff we do now?"

"It's for the story."

Isaac braced himself against the wall. Alyssa, the deserter, was smart enough to leave the girls bathroom window open. The boys could reach it by climbing up on the electric transformer box and leaning over.

"But we can't like go to jail, right?" Cameron clarified.

"You're the valedictorian, I'm the morning news anchor. If we get caught we're probably looking at a week's detention, tops. Slap on the wrist."

"I can't let my college applications have a detention on my transcripts."

"Do they put that kinda stuff on there?" Isaac wondered.

"I'm not sure, but I can't have that on my permanent record."

"We'll be in and out," Isaac said. "But if you want to back out now, I'm fine with that too." Isaac was very fine with backing out. *Please back out*, he tried to will Cameron's next words.

"I think we've got an opportunity here," Cameron said. "How often do eighth graders actually uncover, with real tangible proof, that their teachers are trying to screw over their students?"

"It could be big news," Isaac agreed. "If we find anything."

"We have to. We're going to look back on our lives one day as fifty-year-old men, and we're going to wonder if we ever took any risks. I don't want to pass up this *window* of opportunity."

"Oh that was a good one."

"Yeah, I thought of it just now," Cameron said. "Symbolism."

They looked up at the girls' bathroom window. Neither wanted to admit just how scared they were. But this is how people get real news. That's how they decided to go in. They were there for the story, and that's all. There is a good chance inside they will find something the teachers' lounge.

And forget Alyssa Sonoma.

Except even as Isaac thought this, he knew he was lying to himself. *I mean how does a kid just flat out go and forget the prettiest girl in school wants nothing to do with you? Especially one he's been crushing on her for like six full months?*

Without another impulse in his brain, Isaac leaned forward over the electric box and stretched his hand out to the ledge of the bathroom window. He wished he did it in one smooth fluid motion, but his feet struggled to find a grip against the school's brick wall. He muscled himself up over the ledge.

"You got it?" Cameron asked.

"Wait a sec," Isaac grunted.

"Do you need help?" Cameron said lifting one of Isaac's feet over his head for support. It wasn't until after Isaac received the boost from Cameron that he answered.

"Okay. I got it."

Isaac hung with his butt and legs out the window and his head inside the dark girls' bathroom.

"Ouch, ouch, ouch," Isaac squirmed as his stomach pinched against the raised track of the window. He swung one leg around to get through. He scraped his skin against the windowpane. In the movies, no one ever mentions how it hurts to scrape their skin. *Maybe by the time you are professional like James Bond, those guys are so tough they just ignore that kind of pain.*

Isaac winced to himself getting his final leg through and sort of just fell down on to the bathroom floor. Overall, he convinced himself it was a very smooth entry.

"Are you okay?" Cameron whispered up to the window.

"Throw me the bag, I need a flash light."

On Cameron's fourth attempt, the backpack landed directly on the windowsill. The strap dangled over the ledge low enough that Isaac could pull it down. Isaac tried to ignore the relief that washed over him when the flashlight turned on. The dark is scary.

"Are you coming?" Isaac asked to the window.

"I don't know if I can make the jump," Cameron realized.

At this exact moment, if they were caught, only one of them gets in trouble. Isaac prayed Cameron didn't consider backing out right then. Cameron did consider it for just a few seconds.

"I can let you in through the side door," Isaac offered. He wasn't going to down alone, that's for sure.

"Switching to radio," Isaac said pulling out his walkie-talkie.

They both imagined they were being discreet. But there is nothing quiet about two boys yelling at each other through a window in the dark.

"Mine was in the backpack too. Can you throw it to me?"

"Okay, here it comes," Isaac said.

He shot-put the radio through the window and heard the loud metallic *GLUNG* as the walkie-talkie bounced off the metal electric box.

"Okay, got it," Cameron said. "Switching to radio."

Isaac approached the side door. Having never been in school so late at night, Isaac didn't anticipate that all the lights would be off. For some reason when he walked through it in his head, there was going to be better lighting. At this time of night, the only lights in the school were the emergency exits, and a few spotlights at the end of each hallway. This was wrong. Definitely wrong, and Isaac already felt like he was going to be in a lot of trouble.

And screw Alyssa. So that jerk-bag, high school guy texts her and she just leaves in the middle of a heist? That's it. Get over her, Isaac said to himself as he approached the side door to let Cameron in.

Isaac tried to scan the door for any indications as to whether the fire alarm would go off. There was the red and white emergency pull-tab. He knows not touch that. And then there's that siren thing at the top over the door, protected by the steel wire cage. What's that cage really doing up there anyways? Did some kid somewhere bash in the fire alarm siren so now in all the schools they have to cover them with the steel cage? Or is it just meant to be terrifying? Maybe it's a subconscious reminder to any kid who ever pulls the fire alarm or opens up an emergency exit door as a prank that they're going to find themselves behind bars. That's what Isaac thinks it's there for.

"Oh gosh," Isaac hesitates.

He eyed down the long horizontal push button across the middle of the door. Isaac knew exactly what sound, the loud double-click *CLONK*, he'd hear when he pressed the bar to open the door. That's all Isaac hoped to hear. *If that freakin' alarm goes off, I'm running. I'll run right over Chen too if he's standing too close to the door when it opens.*

"Don't look at it," Isaac said to himself about the fire alarm siren.

CUUSSSHHH!

"Where are you? Over."

CUUSSSHHH!

The walkie-talkie startled Isaac. He nearly jumped out of his socks. Heart racing, he breathed long and slow through his nose.

"Risk takers take risks," he said to himself.

Isaac popped the side door and there was no alarm sound.

Mmph, Isaac thought to himself looking at Cameron waiting patiently at the threshold. *That was almost disappointing. Kinda too easy.*

"I thought the alarm might go off," Cameron whispered. "But I didn't know if you'd think of that and didn't want to make you nervous."

"We were going to have to walk out a door eventually, did you think of that?" Isaac asked.

Cameron curled his index finger around his lips and said, "Actually I didn't." Cameron exhaled. "This heist stuff really requires thinking of all the angles, doesn't it? Really makes you appreciate the movies."

"Let's just hurry up and get this over with."

CH 32

The two boys walked the halls of Pines Lakes Academy thousands of times and figured they'd know where everything was even if they were blindfolded. However, creeping around in the dark with only a few random lights on made the school feel as foreign as if being in the building for the first time. Cameron actually took a wrong turn down the hallway to the teacher's lounge. The real risk came when there was a light on in a classroom. They snuck down along the side of the wall, and approached with extreme caution, signaling to each other with their index fingers over their mouths to be quiet. But there was no teacher in any of classrooms. Someone forgot to turn the light off on the way out.

When Isaac noticed his former 4th grade classroom was also left vacant with the lights on, he couldn't fight off the temptation to walk into the room to look around.

"What are you doing?" Cameron asked in a shushed whisper.

"I just wanna check it out real quick." Isaac said.

"That's not part of the plan."

Isaac took two steps into the room.

"People get caught when they veer off the plan," Cameron reminded Isaac.

"You're right," Isaac shrugged and backed out of the room. "Eyes on the prize."

When they turned the next corner, they practically bumped right into the vacuum cleaner and the custodian holding it. She was a middle-aged woman, shorter than both of them, and probably about as heavy as the two of them combined. The feeling of being dropped in a bucket of ice water hit Cameron and Isaac simultaneously.

There was enough tension in the room to register on a barometer. The custodian wears an old headset, connected to an ancient CD player. She lowers the yellow plastic from her head, and gives the two boys a blank stare.

They are not supposed to be here.

Has she ever seen students in the building this late? Is this normal her for? Why isn't she saying anything? Oh my gosh! We're screwed. We're screwed. We're screwed! All of this repeats through Cameron's head.

Isaac opens his mouth like a reflex reaction. He can feel his jaw moving but he has no idea where these words are coming from. He has never been a good liar. *From where are these falsities coming?*

"We have an extra credit project. We had to stay late," Isaac sort of shouts over the screaming vacuum.

"Okay," the custodian shrugs in a thick accent.

"Yeah, and it's in the teacher's lounge," Cameron adds as they walk away from the exit further down the hall. "We just need to go turn in our homework."

The custodian already put her headphones over her ears and resumed the noise of the vacuum cleaner.

"That was quick thinking," Cameron says.

They tried to walk at a normal stride the rest of the way to the teachers' lounge, but the low lighting made them want to crouch. Isaac pulls out his student ID. He knows it will work. He's used it many times so that he and Cameron could access the teachers' lounge to print documents for the news. So many times. They have absolutely no reason to worry about that now. But because it was dark and after school hours, all the sudden, they worry whether the IDs are going to work.

Cameron raises an eyebrow. Isaac waives his ID over the black module and watches as the small little red light blinks approvingly to green with a beep. They can even hear the door unlock itself.

Isaac exhales, in the nose and out the mouth, like they say in yoga. *Stay calm.* He presses down on the handle and the teacher's lounge door opens. Cameron turns the light on a little too fast. It ruins the moment a bit for Isaac. He wanted that dark dangerous heart fluttering intensity to last just a second longer, but Cameron was too nervous to deal with the stress. Cam flung on the lights and walked in, knowing exactly where he needed to go.

"Without doing the whole thing of trying to make feel me dumb, can you just tell me exactly what you want to find?" Isaac whispered.

Cameron responded in his normal conversational volume. Isaac practically jumped out of his shoes with how loud Cameron spoke. Cameron did this intentionally. Cameron believed that if he could convince himself they weren't doing anything wrong, and acted as normally as he possibly could, then maybe he wasn't actually committing a crime. Maybe, if he turned the light on as soon as he walked into the room, it would hide the fact he broke into the teachers' lounge. And maybe if he spoke at a full volume, he had no reason to believe he was about to steal something.

"We just want to count all of the ballots one more time and compare them to the number of kids in the school. I think there were more ballots than students, and I think that's because the teachers voted."

"What if you're wrong?"

"Then we better get the hell out of here as fast as possible."

"Agreed. Mr. Stentson's desk is over here. The ballots should be in his filing cabinet."

Isaac jiggled the handle; the cabinet was locked. Cameron scoured Stentson's desk. He picked up and moved a few pieces of paper and opened some drawers.

"What are you looking for?"

"This."

Cameron held up a small black key he found in Mr. Stentson's top drawer. He gave it to Isaac, and Isaac inserted the key into the lock. A perfect match. Finally it clicked, and Isaac knew the lock popped. He opened the file cabinet. The green filing folders separated into sections by year, with the most current year first. The green separator contained a blue folder labeled for each grade, sixth through eighth. Isaac pulled out all of them. The folder for each grade had a manila package envelope labeled for each classroom.

"This is it," Isaac whispered.

Cameron looked around; peaking down the hall to make sure no one was coming. Cameron unfolded a piece of paper from his pocket.

"This is the list of every homeroom teacher and the amount of kids in each class. If we're right, and the teacher's voted, then these numbers won't add up."

The boys went through each homeroom counting the number of scantrons in each folder. It was hard to count with a racing heart and the fear that somewhere some ominous timer was ticking down closer to zero. They were trespassing, and the longer they stayed it seemed like the closer they'd come to getting caught. On top of that stress, they each had parents to deal with. It was getting dangerously close to either of them being out way too late on a school night.

And screw Alyssa for ditching me! Isaac reminded himself.

Stacks of scantron ballots lay sprawled out over Mr. Stentson's desk. The boys counted and recounted each classroom, and every single time, the numbers were off. Every time, the vote was higher than what the should have been for each homeroom, by one or in some cases two extra ballots.

"I cant believe this," Isaac said. "This is like a real story."

"The teachers totally fixed the election," Cameron said.

"But how does only one extra vote from each room affect the outcome? We thought Moose would win by a landslide."

"I think I figured that out," Cameron held up a scantron. "Look. The teachers used red pens. Kids vote in pencil. Somehow they must have the machine count only the ballots filled out with a red pen."

Cameron took his phone out, and pulled up the video icon. "Okay, hurry up, are you ready? I'm rolling now. We'll edit later."

"Good evening Pine Lakes Academy, if you don't recognize the background here today, it's because you've never been in this room before. I'm inside the teachers' lounge where a massive conspiracy has been uncovered. Here before me are the scantron ballots for the student body class president . . ."

Cameron moved the camera off of Isaac and while Isaac continued speaking, Cameron panned over the desk with all the scantrons filled out, and then zoomed in on some of them filled out in red pen. Cameron panned back up to put Isaac centered on the frame.

Then, Isaac explained that they uncovered undeniable proof that the teachers rigged the election.

The door beeped behind Isaac.

The handle turned, and from just the outside right boarder of the frame on camera, assistant principal Ms. Lungar entered the shot.

CH 33

Cameron flinched so hard at the sight of Lungar walking through the door that he dropped his phone. Isaac's skin burned fast from his feet all the way to the top of his skull. The blood rushed through his entire body so quickly. Isaac knew not only his cheeks, but his entire body glowed red. He could hardly breath from the shock. They were caught, literally red-handed.

Ms. Lungar didn't enter the room completely. She stood leaning against the doorframe. Her eyes scanned slow over Isaac, Cameron and the spread of scantrons over the desk. She was wearing snug black pants, the seams of which were holding on for dear life, and a red and blue patterned shirt. The red and blue colors acted like police lights in Cameron and Isaac's minds.

Inside Isaac's head, in the submarine control room, his captain and the sailors rattled around while a red siren light and an emergency bullhorn drowned out all other sounds and colors. "Warning! Warning! You are screwed! You are screwed!" The alarm repeated over the submarine cabin. Water flooded the floors and rose quickly.

"Is that still rolling?" Lungar asked Cameron with a nod under the desk. "Pick it up and turn it off."

Cameron reached under the desk to grab the phone he dropped out of nervousness and turned off the recorder. For a half second he wished he could stay under the desk and hide, or maybe just lie down and die of shame right there. His mom will kill him when he gets home anyways, what would an extra twenty minutes be worth at this point?

Cameron stood up with the phone and flashed it to show he turned off the recording.

Lungar leaned off the door and took two steps in to the room. She sat down on the couch chair on the opposite side of the office. She crossed her legs and examined her fingers on one hand while she spoke.

"Well?" She paused. "What the duck is all this?"

Except she didn't say "duck." They'd never heard a teacher say *that* word before. This probably wasn't a good sign, Cameron guessed.

"Ms. Lungar, don't be mad. Listen, you're not going to believe this," Isaac started. "Look at this." Isaac lifted a handful of scantrons, some of them flying and fluttering to the ground like those helicopter seed things from trees.

"We think some of the teachers rigged the election, and we can prove it," Isaac said. "This is a big time news story."

So far, Ms. Lungar didn't seem impressed at all. Cameron noticed she didn't smile, or raise her eyebrows, or ask any questions. In fact, at the mere mention of the idea the election was rigged, Ms. Lungar didn't even flinch. Cameron chimed in here and there to add color commentary and clarify his own hypothesis as to exactly how the teachers were able to manipulate the votes by only counting the red pens. Cameron also added how he developed this theory first when he heard that Mr. Stentson gave the wrong number of votes live on camera. Then, of course, they had the incriminating footage of Ms. Bescomb filling out her own scantron and putting it into the envelope.

After hearing the full explanation, Ms. Lungar clapped her hands. She clapped slow and without any expression. After maybe only four or five depressed claps she said, "You didn't listen to Mr. Docker, did you?"

The question crawled like spiders on both Isaac and Cameron's necks.

"He told you to leave this one alone, didn't he?"

"But Ms. Lungar, this is—"

"—Didn't he say don't cover this one?" Ms. Lungar's face was red. She actually yelled. Her deep, usually friendly voice, sounded like a pit bull's bark with the three of them alone in what was now suddenly feeling like a smaller and darker room.

"Didn't he tell you to leave it alone?" she barked again.

"But Ms. Lungar the votes were—"

"—Fixed. I know they were," Lungar answered. "You two want to come in here and break the law? Disobey orders and act like *real journalists*? You want to be treated like real adults? Fine. I think you earned it. I'm impressed to be honest. So I'm going to do something I've never done before. I'm going to talk to you two like adults. Okay?"

Not okay, not okay. Cameron panicked.

"Yes. I knew the election was decided by the faculty. It was my idea."

"What?" Both Isaac and Cameron thought.

"Do you think the faculty would let you tweens elect that moron president over someone like Glenda?"

Cameron pulled at his hair. This is not how he expected this confrontation to go. What troubled him the most however, was not necessarily the epiphany that Ms. Lungar was apparently in on the whole thing, or being honest to them about it, but that it was still very unclear whether he was actually in any sort of disciplinary trouble yet.

"Listen guys," Ms. Lungar said. "Someone like Glenda is going to put this on her academic resume and it's one of a hundred things that will springboard her to an Ivy League education. Do you think us teachers would strip that away from her to give to some buffoon who doesn't even want the job?"

"But the students voted," Isaac said. And without saying it out loud, he put the facts together. Ms. Lungar's confession was, in a roundabout way, proving that Isaac did indeed run a successful campaign to get Moose elected president. He already wanted to say "I told you so" to Cameron. *Gosh, I am good!* Isaac said to himself. *I can't wait to rub this in Cam's face. If we get out of here alive.*

"We don't care who the kids elected," Ms. Lungar said. "This is our job. Us teachers get paid to be here, we're not letting some tweens screw up our day jobs. And most years, we let you kids pick whoever you want. But sometimes, you make the wrong choice. And I had a feeling this year was going to be one of them."

"But it's the student body president," Cameron chimed in. Realizing now exactly what he was listening to: the teacher's overruled the students' votes. The entire election was just a sham. *Oh gosh,* Cameron thought to himself. *This means Isaac was right and got Moose elected? I hope he doesn't realize that yet.*

"The student body is just a bunch of kids. Do you realize some of those brats who voted for Moose or Macie still believe in Santa?" Ms. Lungar stood. "I'm not letting those idiots tell me how to do my job. Besides, Moose would completely neglect his duties, and you know who would end up doing all the work?"

Ms. Lungar didn't have to answer, they both knew who would end up covering all the required presidential duties.

"So, we decided this year, there was a very clear and deserving candidate. And regardless of the outcome, we knew this candidate was going to be the one who ended up doing the job anyways. So we held a vote. Two options, A for Glenda, B or C for the students' choice. 63% of the teachers in the building wanted Glenda. Easy."

"So the whole election, the campaigns, the debates, everything, that was just a waste of time?" Cameron asked.

"I said I'd talk to you like adults. So yes. It was all a waste. This year. We don't always do this. But come on. You two are smart guys. You think a building full of adults is going to let 400 kids tell us the right thing to do? This isn't a popularity contest. It's an academic position."

[Deleted additional dialog here about how Ms. Lungar was in a similar position at their age. That she was a better candidate but lost to an undeserving imbecile. How she's a better administrator and more responsible adult than the idiots she used to have at her school growing up.]

Isaac scratched his head. Cameron hadn't moved. All Cameron processed so far was that Lungar did not definitively administer a punishment yet.

"This is how life works: We let you children put on your little shows and keep everyone distracted, feel like they're involved—you know that's good for the school environment—but the educated responsible adults make the decisions. We simply could not let someone like Moose or Macie take this away from someone like Glenda. It's the way of the world. Do you two realize that Macie still is convinced she won? She came in third."

"And don't think I don't know," Ms. Lungar continued, "You two were pulling the strings behind Moose the whole way. You should be very proud of yourselves. You brainwashed or peer-pressured—or whatever word you want to use—to convince a very good amount of students to vote for Moose over Glenda, who was clearly a better candidate."

Isaac looked over to Isaac for the "I told you so" moment he'd been waiting weeks to happen. Under the circumstances, it didn't feel as great as he'd hoped, but still it was a rewarding sensation for his ego.

"Isaac, you probably would have won if it was allowed. You're a sharp guy. Almost as smart as Cameron here. But, I don't like either of you two, which is why I'm being honest."

"Well, what is everyone going to say now?" Cameron asked.

"Come on, Mr. Chen," Ms. Lungar said. "I just said you were smart. You already know what happens now."

"We're not running this story?" Cameron said. He rubbed his temples. "This like Big Brother censorship for real."

"Mr. Chen, you and Ms. Howard are probably the only two kids in this school who've read that book. Maybe Ms. Vernar."

"What book?" Isaac asked.

"See?" Ms. Lungar pointed to Isaac. "So here's the deal, you two. Since you really want to be adults in here and act like real journalists, I'm going to cut a deal. I want you to understand how real life works, so here's what we're going to do: If you run this story, I'll have you suspended for breaking into the teachers' lounge, stealing from Mr. Stentson's desk, and it will be enough that your suspension will also strip you of your PLAN privileges. It'll be the last story you tell."

"That's not fair!" Isaac blurted.

"No, it's not fair. It's life." Ms. Lungar said. "I know Mr. Docker told you to leave this story alone, but you wanted to be real life journalists, you wanted to be the media, so here's your chance to be the news."

"So were supposed to lie? To our audience?"

"Hasn't Mr. Docker taught you the most important lesson about television?"

Isaac looked over to Cameron, whose hair was in full handstand mode.

"Tomorrow's Friday. You won't run the story tomorrow, you'd be risking it dies over the weekend. This is a Monday morning story. Yes, I know a little about the news myself.

[Deleted tangent monologue in which Ms. Lungar discussed at length her experience in college as a news reporter. It can be inferred from her story that in actuality, it sounded as if she merely announced one sporting event. However, from this experience she lectured on the intricacies of media, and the importance of timing the delivery of story.]

"You'd have the whole week for it to snowball and takeover the halls. Take the tape home, keep the footage. Think about it over the weekend and decide." Ms. Lungar pulled out her phone and snapped a picture of Isaac and Cameron. "Now, I have a picture of you two breaking in here. So pack it up, and I'm curious to see what you want to do."

"This is B.S.," Isaac said.

"Language, Mr. Budgies. I think you'll end up doing the right thing," Ms. Lungar said and left. "I'm going to call Mr. Docker tonight and fill him in."

The door shut behind Ms. Lungar, leaving Isaac and Cameron staring at each other in complete shock. Then the door re-opened and Lungar walked back in, stepping through Isaac and Cameron and grabbing an empty casserole dish out of the sink.

"Almost forgot this thing again; It was the whole reason I came in here in the first place," Ms. Lungar said. "Guys, keep one thing in mind throughout all this: I'm proud of you and impressed you figured this out. But it's like I said, if you're smart and clever enough to figure this out, then I think you're wise and mature enough to know why it had to be done. You two grew up tonight. Don't sweat it."

CH 34

Like a reptile, Mr. Docker acted totally normal the next day. If he spoke to Lungar, it was completely unnoticeable. On the other hand, Isaac felt like Zoe would need to use some sort of special filter on his cheeks so his face didn't show pure red on camera. Docker went about his routine like there was nothing out of the ordinary while Isaac tiptoed and stewed in rage around the studio. Cameron didn't speak at all. He sat in the corner twitching both of his feet.

Wasn't Docker worried? Budgies wondered to himself. Mr. Docker was about to let Isaac get on camera. Mr. Docker knew Isaac could have used that platform right then and there to shout it from the mountaintops: Ms. Lungar admits the teachers fixed the election! Isaac could tell every kid in school by 8:20 AM. Yet Docker didn't flinch.

Worse than that though, Alyssa strolled into the morning news briefing with an obviously different and apologetic mood. Normally, she'd say good morning to no one. Today, she was chipper and nice to everyone. *What a phony.*

"How'd everything go last night?" she asked Isaac. Like a dog that knew it did something bad, she tried to overcompensate. Since when did she ever ask Isaac anything?

"Fine."

"Did we get what we need?"

We? She's saying 'we' now? Isaac thought, fuming. *This chick.*

"Not really," Isaac said.

"Why are you like being weird today?" Alyssa asked. "Did we get the votes or not?"

Isaac opened his mouth to tell her off. He got as far as separating his lips to make that very unique sound of the spit separating between them, breaking the seal, and inhaling. He puffed his chest, wrinkled his eyebrows, and was ready to let it rip. But in a split second, he decided not to. He shut his mouth and didn't say anything. But Alyssa, knowing what she did the night before was wrong, felt the power in that warning shot. She turned away to end the conversation.

"Okay, do we have any last minute changes we need to put in?" Mr. Docker asked at the morning prep meeting.

He always asked this on Fridays, but today it felt more like a threat. Cameron thought so at least, since Mr. Docker stared right at him while he asked.

And then Ms. Lungar entered the studio, "Just here to watch," she said to the group. And then she motioned her index and middle fingers to her eyes and pointed them at Cameron and Isaac. If Cameron ate anything in the last 12 hours, it probably would have been enough for him to throw up.

Jenny Towel's eyes shot to Isaac, to Cameron, to Zoe, to Mr. Docker, Ms. Lungar, back to Isaac, to Alyssa, to Cameron, and back to Isaac again. But the last one to Isaac was a non-news related glance.

Isn't anyone going to say something? Jenny thought to herself. *Nothing? Unbelievable. Those four are keeping this to themselves. Well, they aren't the only investigative journalists in the room.*

Jenny raised her hand in the meeting. "I was online last night, and there is a crazy rumor going on that the vote investigation is still happening."

Cameron slapped his own forehead.

"Is it?" Mr. Docker asked Jenny while looking at Ms. Lungar, then to Cameron.

"No it isn't," Isaac said to Jenny, hoping she would take the hint. But Isaac denied Jenny for weeks; she was impervious to hints.

FLASH!

A quick bolt of electricity swept across Isaac's mind. It was an idea, an inclination, a connection. He was just about to draw a world-shattering comparison between him constantly shutting down Jenny Towlel and something or someone else. Unfortunately, the urgency of making sure Jenny didn't say something to get him fired overtook his primary brain functions. *Oh well, it probably wasn't important.*

"Yes, Isaac," Jenny continued. She perked up in stance now, perhaps excited maybe she was the first to get her hands on a juicy rumor. "People are saying that you—that someone, I mean—is still looking into the recount."

"And what are they saying about the recount?" Ms. Lungar asked. "Isaac, did you hear about this?"

"I did," Alyssa said.

Cameron coughed or choked or something; he made some kind of disgusted noise to himself. Alyssa was going rogue.

Not to be outdone, Jenny divulged even more information, "Yeah, so like a lot of people have heard that there may have been a miscalculation in the votes. And that people are saying Moose won."

"And who are the students looking into this?" Ms. Lungar asked Jenny.

Gosh what a pro, Zoe thought to herself. Zoe of course knew everything from Cameron. She watched

Ms. Lungar cross examine Jenny like a state's attorney with an excited witness. Jenny was spilling the beans! Only because in her mind she was showing off, not realizing she just fell into a maniacal tyrant's web of a trap.

"It's Isaac and Cameron," Jenny volunteered.

"We didn't go," Isaac whispered out of the side of his mouth to Jenny.

Oh! She thought to herself, realizing she just made big mistake by opening her mouth.

"You guys still think the votes were wrong?" Ms. Lungar asked them. "Didn't we watch the recount on the live news? I vaguely remember being there." Lungar puckered her lips, letting everyone in the room know it was time to laugh at her joke.

"We're looking into it," Alyssa said. Trying to keep her hands on this story as much as she could at this point.

"Have you found anything yet?" Mr. Docker asked Isaac. "I didn't know this rumor already started."

"I didn't know that either," Isaac said honestly. "We're not sure. We need more time."

Zoe folded her hands in front of her mouth. No one else in the room knew the subtitles of these undertones. *What a show*. The camera guys, Jenny, Alyssa, they had no idea what they were missing right now.

"Best to stay in front of rumor. Isaac, I want you to give an update. Let the students know this is an ongoing investigation. Don't let it get out of control," Lungar said. "But I don't want to tell you how to do your job."

"Okay," Isaac said. He puffed his chest out to Alyssa. She didn't know how far out of the story she had been pushed. *Maybe she never will*, he decided.

"Agreed," Cameron said.

📷 📷 📷

Looking straight into the lens, surprisingly not nervous at all, Isaac added, "And a quick update: In response to the growing allegations regarding the student body president voting recount, we do want to submit a clarifying report that a team of Pine Lakes Academy News correspondents have started an initial investigation, but currently there is nothing further to report at this time. Jenny, is it true the cafeteria isn't going to serve any deserts on Mondays anymore?"

That's how to bury something.

Mr. Docker taught Isaac how to do bury stories last year.

"If you mention it, if you throw it out there like it's so boring that you're worried your audience is going to change the channel if you talk about it for one second longer, they'll ignore it." He was right. If the news anchor doesn't care about something, neither will the audience.

Mr. Docker also said, "People watch the news to be entertained first, informed second. Remember, if it's not on the news, it's not important. People will think if it's not on the front page, it's not a big deal."

Well, Isaac just let perhaps the biggest bombshell of a story he'd ever known slide out into oblivion. Now, all anyone will be talking about is whether its true that the cafeteria did or did not serve deserts on Mondays. Even after Jenny explained there will be desserts. In one ear and out the other. And it worked. Isaac wanted to take a shower.

📹 📹 📹

"Hi, Isaac," Glenda said in the hallway.

Here it comes. I've been threatened enough this week.

"Hey, Glenda. What's up?"

"Oh, I've just been really busy working on this English paper. Have you started yours yet?"

"Yeah, I mean, sort of. It's not due until—"

"—Anyway Isaac, what did you mean today about the 'ongoing investigation' with the votes? I thought that was done, isn't it? Am I class president or not?"

Glenda brushed her hair from her face using four fingers. Her eyes were puffy and cheeks flushed.

Probably, she was up all night working on her English paper that wasn't due for two more weeks. Then she woke up early to go to some club's meeting before school. And after all that, she watched the morning news to find out there was still some nosey kid trying to take her title form her. She wasn't on the group chats last night wasting her time like Jenny Towlel. Glenda found out this morning.

"Oh it's, nothing Glenda," Isaac lied.

"Isaac, I am the student body president. Elected by my peers. If there's an ongoing investigation into whether I won, I need to know. I thought this was over already? I can't have my name smeared around in some scandal, what if the teachers lose respect for me?"

"Glenda, trust me, I don't think that's the problem."

"Well is there someone still looking into the votes? Is there a problem? I mean what else is there to even look at? We already counted them, right?"

Before Isaac could answer, she asked, "Is it you? Are you the one investigating?"

"Um, listen. We just wanted to run with this story through the week. Adults are always talking about recounts and stuff, so we thought we could play it out longer."

"Really? That's it?"

"Yes, we wanted to make sure each ballot was counted by hand."

"That doesn't sound like a very compelling controversy," Glenda said. "But I agree, I guess. The votes should be correct. It's paramount the voice of the people is heard. I want to make a statement supporting the manual count."

Glenda pulled out her phone to make an official tweet.

"I don't think you should do that."

"Why not?"

"Well, it's the end of the week. Fridays are a good time to refresh the news cycle. Don't want to stir up any more controversy, I'd think. Don't you agree?"

Glenda holstered her phone. "You're probably right. But Isaac, will do you me a favor?"

"Sure what's up?"

"Can you text me once this is officially over? I think as president, I deserve the right to find out before I have to hear about it on the morning news, don't you agree?" She was using his words now.

"But Glenda, what if you didn't win?"

"Oh my gosh, I didn't win?"

"No, no. I'm just saying, let's say we find out that maybe you didn't win. Would you still want to know if you lost?"

Glenda breathed through her noise.

"Isaac, I didn't run for president as a popularity contest, or as a joke. I ran because I love this school. I have a lot of good policy ideas that will last for years after I'm gone. If I'm not the president, then it's the school's loss."

"But what if like, you did lose, and I'm the only one who knew? Would you want me to report the story?"

"Off the record," Isaac added.

"Off the record or not, I'd still tell you to do the same thing,"

"And what's that?"

"The right thing."

CH 35

"You guys are so screwed," Zoe said in Cameron's basement. It was Saturday afternoon.

Zoe sat on the couch at the very tip end of her seat. Cameron sprawled spread eagle on his back on the carpet floor, his hair crawling out in all directions as far away from his head as possible. Isaac with his arms crossed and one hand over his mouth stared out the window. This is how the dudes in the movie looked when they were contemplating, and he hoped he was doing it right.

"I've spent a quarter of my life building a career as a news producer," Cameron said.

Zoe rolled her eyes.

"I can't have that taken away from me."

"But you took a vow as a reporter to tell the news," Zoe said. "You have to get this out. The students have the right to know. It's your duty as a news teller to get the truth out."

"Zoe, I could get suspended."

"Cameron who cares? We are going to school under suppressive fascist rule. Ms. Lungar has no right to control our elections."

"Who did you vote for, Zoe?" Cameron asked.

"Glenda, of course. She's the most qualified. Same with you, right?"

"Yeah. So, you would rather Glenda lose the election and have Moose be the school president?"

"Well, no. Moose is a joke, Glenda definitely should have won."

"So, then you agree with Lungar?" Cameron said.

"I agree that Glenda should have won, Cameron. But I don't agree with Lungar having the ability to unilaterally strike down the voice of the student body. You can't let them get away with this! It's like unconstitutional, probably."

"Zoe, if we tell this story, we get suspended and we're kicked off the broadcast team. I can't give that up," Cameron said looking up at the ceiling fan.

"I thought you were braver than this," Zoe said. "Docker isn't going to kick you off the broadcast. Who's going to replace you? No one can do your job."

"You could," Cameron admits.

"Well yeah, he probably would have me take over. I could definitely do your job. But so what? You have to take a stand."

"Then why don't you break the story if you're so hot about it?"

"Me? No," Zoe says. "I can't get involved in this. It's your own problem."

"What do you think over there?" Cameron asked Isaac. "Do we tell the truth or go along with Ms. Lungar and keep our jobs and stay out of trouble?"

Isaac didn't answer.

"Budgies, what are you thinking?" Zoe asked.

"I mean what does she even see in that guy?" Isaac said.

"Dude!"/"Come on!" They both responded in unison.

"You're facing serious disciplinary charges, and risking your anchor chair but you can only think about some dumb girl?" Zoe asked.

"We were right there, she was at the fence. Then she gets a text? And now what? You abandon us at the gate?"

"Okay, you want to just talk about this? Let's do it," Zoe said.

"Kind of."

"Then here it is," Cameron said. "You got dumped."

"Dumped? That's like a total desertion," Zoe said. "She doesn't like you, man. Hard truth."

"Agreed. It's not going to happen," Cameron said. "Ever. Hard truth."

"But why aren't I good enough for her?" Isaac asked. "You guys don't get it. Like I like her, but I'm not good enough for her to like me back."

"No one is good enough for her," Cameron said.

"Okay, two things," Zoe said. "Number one: she is not too good for you. She is literally the worst person I know. But I get it. You're like thirteen and your hormones are like Chernobyl right now. It's impossible for you to make rational decisions. You just see that padded bra and 'Oh look, Isaac's brain is flying away!' I understand. You think she's hot."

"You just need to get over her, once and for all. She stranded us at the fence. She's no journalist," Cameron added.

"And secondly," Zoe added. "Let's just say for one second that maybe she is better than you, okay? Like why is your ego so shattered that you aren't up to her standards? Are you Percy Jackson? Are you Ron Weasley? What's so amazing about Isaac Budgies? Maybe you should lower your standards. No offense, but you're not exactly Tony Stark. Not everyone has to like you."

Isaac looked away from the window. He exhaled long and hard. Cameron sat up from the floor. Zoe stood.

"Sorry, was that too harsh?" she asked.

"No it was fine. I know what I have to do now."

"Like as in getting over Alyssa Sonoma and moving on with your life, or about deciding if you are going to get suspended or bury the biggest news story ever?"

Isaac ran up the stairs out of the basement.

"Where are you going?" Cameron asked.

"Hard truth," Isaac shouted. "I'm not mad."

"Call me later," Cameron said as the door shut. Maybe Isaac responded with an okay but it was too hard to hear.

"Was I mean?" Zoe asked again.

"He'll be fine."

"What are you guys going to do?" Zoe asked.

"Sounds like we'll find out tonight."

"Come sit over here," Zoe said.

CH 36

Isaac Budgies thanked his good fortune to find himself pitted against two impossible options. *How many?* He wondered. How many young journalists at his age have already found themselves centered in a web of corruption and injustice? Alyssa Sonoma was a welcome distraction to his current plight. There was one thing that unsettled Isaac most about the conversation with Ms. Lungar in the teachers' lounge. Isaac couldn't describe the emotion he felt throughout the conversation. It was something he was unable to put into words.

The same nagging feeling found returned between his third and fourth ribs while Zoe spoke to him about Alyssa. What was that feeling called? Isaac found that when his conscience was trying to talk to him, he needed to find a quiet place to listen. He needed to turn off his headphones, silence his phone, and get fresh air. He went for a bike ride. There were two stops he needed to make.

"Just get it over with," he said to himself as he peddled harder.

Inside Isaac's mind, several military generals stood around a map inside of a war room bunker. The room was poorly light. A single swinging light bulb hung from the dirt and boarded ceiling.

"This is madness," one of the general's said to the rest. All of the generals were Isaac Budgies. Each of them varied in age, with different outfits and different amounts of dirt or scars on them.

"It's a suicide mission," another of the Isaac Budgies general said.

"We have no choice, we have to attack head on," the bearded and oldest looking general said. He slammed a fist down on the table.

Isaac approached the front door of Alyssa's house and knocked. Each knock sent a static shock through his body and stopped his heart. Then an eternity of time passed.

"Abort! Abort the mission!" a general in Isaac's mind called.

Another general, said, "Be still, man. Keep your wits about you."

Before Isaac had any further chances to freak out, or run away, the maid answered the door.

"For Alyssa?" the maid asked.

Isaac nodded, very surprised at the maid's assumption.

"I'm telling you something's wrong!" the young soldier in the war room urged the others. "How can she possibly know we're here for Alyssa? It's a trap, I say. It's a trap, dammit!"

"Katrina, who is it?" Alyssa's voice called from somewhere up and beyond the double-sided curling entry staircase.

"Here is date," Katrina yelled up.

Date? Isaac questioned.

Then, Alyssa appeared, looking like a beauty pageant contestant. As in she was actually dressed for a beauty pageant. She was wearing a full on evening gown, glitter, make-up that took hours, and her hair was professionally styled. Isaac never felt more attracted to anyone, ever. Suddenly, whatever he wanted to say had been Ctrl+Alt+Del from his mind, and he felt inadequate in his t-shirt and jeans. This was not a good idea to come here.

"Oh, it's just you," Alyssa said. "Katarina, that's not my date!"

Then he realized what happened. She wouldn't have to tell him.

"We've lost," the general said with his head down. The soldiers heard the whistling scream of what was presumably a bomb falling overhead. There were many planes carrying many bombs coming right for them.

The pearlescent emerald green and pink dress changed colors from whichever angle he looked at it. The dress reached down to the floor, but its high slit revealed Alyssa's leg. Completely inappropriate for someone her age, but seeing it left Isaac's mouth dry. The disappointment in her rolling eyes and dropped shoulders at the sight of him, crumbled Isaac's pride. She walked to about halfway down the steps and stopped there. Symbolically, he'd have to call up to her like in a romantic play.

Isaac usually didn't handle directing, but he couldn't help but imagine how he'd shoot the scene. From Alyssa's vantage point, it would be Isaac, standing at the threshold of the front door, self-framed and tight, shot from above. When looking at Alyssa, from Isaac's perspective, he'd use a wide shot, capturing the grandeur of the house. The wide lens could depict his literal lofty goal standing above him.

I can't turn it off, Isaac said to himself. *It'd be a classic scene though. Focus!*

"What do you want?" Alyssa asked from halfway up the steps.

Ew, please leave. Why is he such a stalker? Alyssa shrieked in her own head. This was supposed to be her day. Her spotlight, her story. *If John shows up while he's here, I will be so embarrassed. He better not tell anyone either! Macie is going to like literally die when she sees this dress.*

"Um, nothing," Isaac said.

"Okay, then bye? Thanks."

The dialog did not live up to his production hopes. Isaac made a mental note that life is never as dramatic as the movies. At this point, the battle was lost and the war was over. Isaac finally accepted Alyssa very obviously was not interested in him at all. Yet, he rode all the way over here. *Don't I deserve an explanation?* He thought he did.

The nice thing about losing, if there is anything nice about it, is that a loss is a loss. Losing 100-0 is the same loss as losing 100-99. So Isaac decided if he's turning around and walking out the door with a broken heart, he at least could inquire as to why.

"Well, I just wanted to ask you a question."

"Oh my gosh, Isaac. Is this about the election? Can we just talk about it later? My date is going to be here like any second."

The maid walked back into the room with a corsage. She held it in one hand, with the pin out in the other, and headed towards Isaac with it. She reached out for Isaac's shirt and tried to pin the flower on him.

"Katrina, no! That's not my date."

Isaac pulled away from the flower while the confused maid looked at him shaking her head. She took a few steps off to the side, but did not leave the room. Just in case anyone wasn't already feeling awkward enough, her presence guaranteed the conversation would be as difficult as possible.

"It's not about the election."

"What do you want?"

He could hear himself asking the question. The words boiled inside the bottom of his stomach, and he knew they wanted to come out of his mouth, but it was hard to be vulnerable. His armpits started to sweat.

"I just wanted to know why you don't like me."

"Oh."

Why? Alyssa asked herself. *Why don't I like the most pompous kid in school? Why don't I like the kid who everyone says would be my "perfect match?" Why don't I want to be a spectacle at all times?*

Alyssa asked these questions while also simultaneously realizing to herself that John was equally pompous. That she envied movie stars who dated their on-screen matches. She most certainly did want to be a spectacle at all times. So what was the real reason she didn't like Isaac Budgies?

"Because I want to get to wear this dress to high school homecoming."

The answer surprised both of them, probably because it was honest. To Alyssa's credit, the answer worked because it was an absolute. There was nothing Isaac could take personally. It was a just a fact, a hard truth. He was in 8th grade, and therefore could not take Alyssa to a high school homecoming dance. It wasn't because he wasn't cute enough, or wasn't a good enough athlete, or because he didn't have enough money, or that she didn't like his taste in music. Alyssa did not like Isaac, but she didn't like him for a reason that had little to do with Isaac himself. So, that was more stomachable.

On the other hand, Isaac couldn't help but recoil at such a stupid reason. Could she really be that superficial? She wants to go to homecoming so she can wear a dress? And this affects her on an emotional level? The reaction is enough to choose a guy, basically any guy, as long as he was in high school? Suddenly, the spell was broken.

If her reasoning for not liking me is going to be based on something so shallow, then maybe Cameron and Zoe have been right the whole time. And there was that same weird feeling in his ribs again.

One of them would have to say something now, and it was Isaac's turn to speak.

"Cause you want to wear a dress?"

"Yeah, okay? Pretty much. He's in high school; you're not. I'm going to homecoming; you're not. Okay?"

It was okay. Isaac saw now that Alyssa's emotional decisions were tied to material objects. It didn't matter to her that they had a lot in common or that he would treat her well. What mattered to Alyssa Sonoma was wearing a pretty dress, and Isaac couldn't give that to her. It seemed like such a dumb reason not to like somebody. But as his friends tried to tell him, she was dumb.

"Like almost no girls get to go to Homecoming in 8th grade. It's really important to me that I get to go early."

"Yeah, I get it. I guess. Thanks for being honest with me," Isaac said. "I have to go."

"Do you think that's a dumb reason?" she asked.

"I guess being disappointed never has a good reason," he shrugged. "Being disappointed is almost never for the reason that you'd expect, I guess."

"And Isaac," she called after him when he turned for the door. "Next year, when we're both in high school and we can both go to homecoming..."

His heart stood still waiting for hope. Maybe there will be hope. Maybe next year, he'll have a chance.

"John's going to be able to drive," she bit her lower lip after she said it.

"But good luck with the election stuff," she said. *Move on with your life*, is what she meant.

"Have fun at the dance, you look pretty."

"Can you take a picture and send it to Jenny so she can talk about it on her weekend wrap up?"

There it is. The full vanity comes out now. It was like Alyssa opened up to the fact that she was materialistic and superficial, and the floodgates of her shallow depths poured out without shame.

Take a picture of her. Put it on the news; let everyone see how pretty she is. To even have the nerve to ask such a thing! Isaac understood completely, it's why him and her would make such a good pair, but she didn't care.

"No," he said and left.

CH 37

Another hard truth. Isaac left Alyssa's house stewing over her rationale. He'd have to tell Zoe and Cameron about this, of course. But first, he had one more stop to make. With the "Operation Alyssa" put away from his mind, Isaac could finally focus on his bigger problem. Report the news and lose his job as a news anchor, or bury a story but continue reporting the news, the *other* news, just not this one huge, good story.

For the first time all school year, he had a clear head. There wasn't much of a debate for Isaac. He convinced Moose to run and then Isaac ran the campaign for Moose, and easily convinced most of the kids in school to vote for Moose. Moose wasn't qualified at all, but Isaac campaigned him as a shiny new toy, and kids like shiny new things, so Moose won. Should Moose have won? No, he wasn't qualified. Kids are dumb. The teachers, in their vast infinite wisdom, and probably from some of Lungar's deep seeded resentment of Macie, recognized what was going on, and stepped in. The teachers voted to give the president responsibilities to Glenda. Are the teachers wrong? Well, they lied. Lying is wrong. But did Glenda deserve to win? Yes.

But the question is not whether Glenda deserves to win, because she does. Totally, no doubt about it. In fact, Isaac voted for her. But that's not the question; it's whether she did win. And Glenda did not win.

Just then Isaac's phone chirped. It was Cameron. He was texting on the group chat with Isaac, Cameron, and Zoe.

- CAM: whats the plan?
- ISAAC: i think you kno
- CAM: good job
- ZOE: wait, what does that mean?
- CAM: should i say it?
- ISAAC: If you dont know the right thing to do
- ISAAC: do whats harder
- ISAAC: "hard truth"
- ZOE: yay! I KNEW YOU WOULD!
- ISAAC: thx for pep talk
- ZOE: sorry about alyssa stuff :(
- ISAAC: np, i needed it
- ISAAC: I'm at moose house
- ISAAC: gonna give him heads up
- CAM: ☺

Isaac is a reporter. He took a solemn oath as an investigative journalist to tell the truth. So regardless of the circumstance, the truth must be told. "I have . . ."

📷 📷 📷

Isaac went from rehearsing the monolog in his head to reciting it out loud on Moose Patrowski's driveway while Moose was shooting hoops.

"I have a duty to inform the students of Pine Lakes what's going on. I gotta report the news. Ms. Lungar and the teachers overruled the students' choice and they didn't tell us. It's going to be the top headline Monday morning."

Moose stopped dribbling. He didn't speak. He didn't move.

"So that means you won."

No answer.

"Moose, aren't you excited? Say something? I'm saying you actually won the student election. We—I mean—you, you won!"

"No."

"What do you mean no? No what?"

"No, I'm not excited," he said walking over to Isaac. "This is the worst news of my life."

The smile erased from Isaac's face. "What?"

Moose looked around to make sure they were alone in the yard. "I don't want to be president."

"What? Why? What are you talking about, man? This is a huge story. The teachers tried to cover—"

"Shut up."

"Moose?"

"Seriously, I don't want to win. I don't want to be president; it sucks. Ms. Lungar is all over my ass just to do student council. She thinks I'm like a diploma now."

"You mean diplomat?"

"Whatever."

"You don't want to be student president?"

"Are you listening to me, Budgies? No. I don't want to do it. Student council is for nerds, man."

"But Moose?"

"I don't want to go to the meetings. They're in the morning; they're after school; they have stuff going on at lunch. It's like non-stop with that crap. I don't want it. I don't want anything to do with it."

"Are you serious right now?"

"I'm dead serious, let it go. Keep your little bird mouth shut. Glenda is a dork. She's like constantly texting me ideas and projects and crap. It's a nightmare, man. Plus, you'll be hurting her feelings. Did you think of that?"

Isaac never thought about Glenda's feelings. She would be devastated.

"Just leave it. I'll take the loss and move on with my life. Please, dude."

Moose's face was red. Tears actually sat wobbling at the bottom of his eyes, right on the verge of spilling over. Moose was being serious, dead serious.

"Moose, you told me you wanted to look into a recount."

"Dude, I didn't know I'd have to eat every Friday lunch with Ms. Lungar. I can't do it. If you announce it, I'll re-sign myself."

"It's resign. Not *re-sign*."

"I don't freaking care! I'll quit and then Glenda will be the president anyways. So what's the point?"

"The point is I have to report the news."

"Why? You'll announce I win, and then Glenda will cry, and probably hate you. Then I'll quit, then Glenda will do it, but it will suck for her cause then she knows she's like the second choice. You're going to ruin everything and Glenda will still end up president anyways, except worse."

"Those are not bad points," Isaac scratched his head. "What about the teachers, though? They lied to us."

"Who cares? They're adults. They lie to us all the time. Ever heard of Santa Claus? Who cares?"

"Well, what about the story though, like are you going to tell people?"

Moose picked up the basketball again and started dribbling. "Dude, I am so over this nerd stuff, I'm never going to talk about it again."

"What about when all your buddies make fun of you for losing and you try to defend yourself?"

Moose sunk a swish.

"I'm going to say 'I actually I won the election, but the teachers gave it to Glenda Howard instead, and then I found out about it and so did big mouth Isaac Budgies, but he never told anyone.' And no one will believe me."

It was a pretty unbelievable story, especially without any proof. *Well this is a drastic turn of events.* Certainly not the reaction Isaac was looking for.

"But I need to do the right thing," Isaac said.

"Does doing the right thing mean you actually just want to break a big headline news story?"

"No," Isaac said. *Maybe though*, he admitted to himself.

"Please, man. Don't do it. Okay?"

Am I actually getting complex emotional advice from Moose? Isaac couldn't believe the words that were about to come out of his mouth:

"Okay Moose, I think you're actually right."

"So you'll leave it alone?" Moose pumped both of his fists, "I'm done with the dork stuff?"

Isaac let out a long exhale as if releasing a pressure valve. He rubbed his forehead, stopped himself quickly realizing that was what Cameron always does.

"I guess. If that's what you really want? You are technically the president."

CH 38

"If that's what he wants," Cameron agreed.

"No way!" Zoe contested. "You guys have to tell the students!"

"But why?" Isaac asked.

The three of them were back inside Cameron's basement for a Saturday night of watching movies. Probably, somewhere, a group of kids their age were out in a larger group in someone else's basement, partying. Isaac knew Alyssa was dancing the night away in her dress. He tried not to think about that. In high school, he imagined they played nothing but slow songs the entire night and probably her date's suit would smell like her perfume for weeks.

"If the teachers wanted to pick the class president, then they should have announced it. You can't just lie to the students and make us think we're voting if it doesn't matter."

"But Moose doesn't want to be president," Isaac repeated himself.

"So what? He ran; that's his problem. If he doesn't want to be president, then he can step-down."

"Then Glenda will be president," Isaac said. "Which, she already is now. Except she'll get her feelings hurt, and realize she was the second choice."

"Isn't that better than walking around letting her think she won if she really didn't?" Zoe asked.

"Well she did win the teacher's vote," Cameron said. "Which is like adults saying she would do a better a job than Moose."

"Yes, obviously," Zoe conceded. "That's why I voted for her."

"So Zoe, the only people who know that the teachers voted for Glenda are the three of us in this room, and Moose. And Moose doesn't want it. I was all for breaking the story, but if Moose doesn't want to win, then I think we let it be."

"What happened to 'choose the harder path'? I thought you said you were going to do the right thing." Zoe's face started to turn red.

"This is doing the right thing. Not telling the story is the right thing," Isaac said.

"How can you possibly say that?" Zoe yelled.

"Because there's nothing I want to do more than break the news on a teacher's conspiracy! Do you know how famous that would make me? Not telling is the harder choice."

"Oh," Zoe said.

Isaac's honesty threw Zoe for a loop.

"You know, when we were down here earlier today," Isaac said, "I had this weird feeling in my chest while you were talking to me about Alyssa, and saying I needed to get over her because she's never going to like me. It's weird because I had that same feeling while Lungar was telling me why the teachers picked Glenda. And you know what I realized that feeling was?"

"Gas?" Cameron asked.

"No, seriously," Isaac said. "I realized, and this is hard for me to admit, but it was the feeling of me recognizing that I was wrong, and I was changing my mind. It's something I basically never do."

"Wow, you're sick," Zoe's eyes widened.

"But for real. I never admit I'm wrong. But you were right about Alyssa, and Lungar was right about Glenda. I mean, even frickin' Moose said the same thing. So, as much as I want to tell this story, forget it. It's time to grow up."

"But the teachers lied," Zoe said.

"They're adults, who cares?" Cameron asked, weirdly echoing Moose's same thought. "Do you know how much adults lie to kids? Basically all the time."

"So we're just going to let them get away with it?" Zoe asked.

"They didn't get away with it," Isaac said. "We caught them. We know the truth, and they know we know. That's pretty cool."

"I don't agree with this," Zoe said. "But I also don't care."

CH 39

As usual, that Monday morning, Isaac walked into the school building and the first thing he did was try to make a stop in the bathroom. His bathroom, the private one he had access to with his student ID. He swiped his ID, and in one motion pushed down on the handle and put his shoulder into the door like he always did.

SMACK!

His shoulder pounded into the door as if he walked right into a wall. Locked. He swiped the ID several more times to no avail. Cameron's didn't work either.

"Well, that's just not fair," Cameron said. "Can she do that? Can she shut off our IDs?"

"She's sending us a message," Isaac said.

"What's the message?" Cameron asked. "That she wants us to use the trough bathrooms like peasants? That she's an unfair dictator?"

"We abused our privilege, she's punishing us," Isaac said.

"This is unjust. I can't use a public restroom. I haven't used anything but this one in two years."

"I'd say pretty fair trade that we aren't suspended right now," Isaac admitted.

"I'd say this is a travesty and maybe we should spill the beans to the whole school."

"Come on, we're not going to do that. And I think she knows it. The bathroom was a compromise. Let's go."

"How exactly are you going to do it, by the way?" Cameron asked. "Isaac Budgies, the guy with the little birds all over the school? You're not going to tell the biggest story we've ever discovered?"

"I think I'm okay with it."

Cameron looked around as the hustling students trickled in through the doors. Most played outside or clustered in various talking circles. To them, today was just a normal Monday, Glenda Howard was the student body president, and the world was as it always seemed to be. For Cameron, he realized he separated himself from the students. He knew something none of them knew, and Cameron was part of the reason why they'd never know it.

"Look at all them," Cameron said. "They have no idea."

"It's like Lungar said: we're on the other side now, grown up." Isaac patted Cameron's shoulder.

🎥 🎥 🎥

"That is some great work, Jenny. Thank you, very exciting." Isaac said as the camera cut to him. "Alyssa, thank you for sharing that with us. I'm sure it's every 8th grade girl and her parents' dream to get to go to a high school dance a year early."

"Okay, it's now or never. Zoe said from inside the production room."

"He's not—I mean—*we're* not, going to do it," Cameron said.

"I want to go on record that I wanted the truth to be known. But also that I don't care about drama or TV."

"I care about you," Cameron said with a wink. "Do you care about me?"

Zoe rolled her eyes. She smiled, "When you're honest."

"Thank you Isaac and Jenny," Alyssa said to the camera. "It was so much fun. And in related news: seventh and eighth graders, student council is set to announce the date of our school dance later this week. Stay tuned. Isaac."

"Thank you, Alyssa. Speaking of student council, Our PLAN team wrapped up the investigation into any possible recount of the student body presidential vote, and can confirm the results of the election: the correct candidate was selected. We've said it before here, but another congratulations to Glenda Howard."

No hiccups, no pauses, no ums or likes. Another spot-on, flawless delivery from the seasoned veteran. And technically he wasn't lying. The correct candidate was selected, he just didn't say by whom.

"That's the morning news. Tomorrow, we'll tell you what we learned today."

5 YEARS LATER

High school proms usually happen at hotels. Pine Lakes Senior High School held its Prom on a large gala boat. Cameron Chen and Zoe Vernar, still together, both dressed in black, with a black corsage Zoe picked out herself. People tend to get sentimental at grand events like this. For many, prom is a sign of growing up.

Of course, Isaac didn't believe in responding with volatile emotions to moments, but he certainly didn't object to the group shot requested of the old eighth grade Pine Lakes Academy News team. He never spoke to Alyssa anymore, but the group urged the two of them to stand next to each other. Unplanned, Isaac's suit and silver tie complimented perfectly to Alyssa's silver dress. One last reminder to Isaac of what was never meant to be.

Isaac put his other arm around Cameron, his best friend. Jenny Towlel, who was at prom with a senior, stood on the edge. She was too cool to be associated with most of this crowd at this point in her life. But they gathered in, the camera crew too, and someone took a picture.

"We should send this to Mr. Docker," someone joked.

Immediately after the photo, the band started to play a slow song. Glenda Howard was there to admire the old memory and Isaac asked her if she wanted to dance. They both came with other dates as "just friends," so they had no obligations to anyone during a slow song. Glenda's dark black hair tied up over her orange dress, highlighted her smooth dark skin. It didn't matter she was still sporting thick frame glasses; she looked fantastic.

The two talked while they danced, mostly reminiscing about memories that accumulated after junior high, but neither acknowledged they really never ran in the same crowds. Glenda mentioned something about PLAN, which triggered a memory Isaac had long forgotten.

"That reminds me," he said. "I don't know if I should tell you this, but remember the eighth grade election?"

Glenda started giggling. "Oh my gosh. I thought I was so important."

"Well, I actually found out Ms. Lungar and the teachers were the ones who voted for you; the students voted for Moose Patrowski. But Lungar told me you were more responsible and would do a better job, so they gave it to you instead."

Glenda laughed, "Oh my gosh, you knew that?"

Isaac pulled away, "Wait, did you know that?"

"Yeah, of course I knew," she said. "Ms. Lungar told me everything the day before the election."

"And you didn't care?" Isaac asked, a bit thrown off that after all this time, and all the heartache he put into that story many years ago, Glenda knew all along.

"I mean why should I care?" she shrugged. "I didn't want to win a popularity contest, I wanted to be the class president."

Isaac shook his head, "Politicians."

Glenda smirked.

Isaac continued dancing with Glenda until the song ended. But it bothered him very much that he never knew there was more to that story. For a guy whose job it was to know everything, he wondered how much he didn't know.

The End

About the Author

Michael Dave likes jokes. This is his second funny novel. His first book, CAMP TALLAWANDA, was the #1 best selling middle grade lacrosse comedy of 2019. He lives in Chicago, but can often be found on Lake Erie in the summer. Follow him on Instagram, @realmikedave.

Made in the USA
Monee, IL
28 November 2022